YOU ARE ELIZABETH BENNET

Emma Campbell Webster studied English literature at the University of Oxford, where she specialised in Austen. She later worked as an actress in theatre and television before going on to write her first book, *You Are Elizabeth Bennet*. Originally from Norwich, England, she now lives in Los Angeles with her two daughters.

YOU ARE ELIZABETH BENNET

CREATE YOUR OWN
JANE AUSTEN ADVENTURE

EMMA CAMPBELL WEBSTER

faber

This edition first published in the UK in 2025
by Faber & Faber Ltd
The Bindery, 51 Hatton Garden
London EC1N 8HN

First published in the UK in 2007 by Atlantic Books,
an imprint of Grove Atlantic Ltd

Typeset by Faber & Faber Ltd
Printed and bound by CPI Group (UK) Ltd, Croydon, CR0 4YY

All rights reserved
© Emma Campbell Webster, 2007, 2025

The right of Emma Campbell Webster to be identified as author
of this work has been asserted in accordance with Section 77 of
the Copyright, Designs and Patents Act 1988

A CIP record for this book
is available from the British Library

ISBN 978–0–571–39790–7

Printed and bound in the UK on FSC® certified paper in line with our continuing
commitment to ethical business practices, sustainability and the environment.
For further information see faber.co.uk/environmental-policy

Our authorised representative in the EU for product safety is
Easy Access System Europe, Mustamäe tee 50, 10621 Tallinn, Estonia
gpsr.requests@easproject.com

For my mum, Chrissie

CONTENTS

Your Mission
ix

VOLUME ONE
1

VOLUME TWO
69

VOLUME THREE
159

Acknowledgements
227

YOUR MISSION

*I*t is a truth universally acknowledged that a young Austen heroine must be in want of a husband, and you are no exception. Christened Elizabeth Bennet, you are tolerably beautiful, moderately accomplished, with a sharp wit and quick mind. You are the daughter of misguided but well-meaning parents and live with them and your four sisters – Jane, Mary, Kitty and Lydia – in the village of Longbourn, near the town of Meryton. You are of a happy disposition and have hitherto whiled away your years reading, walking and enjoying what limited society Meryton has to offer. A recent event, however, threatens to disturb your tranquillity: a man of large fortune has let a nearby manor house. Inconsequential though this change of circumstance appears, it is the first in a long chain of events that will require you to face difficult decisions and impolite dance partners. Equipped with only your wit and natural good sense, your mission is to marry both prudently and for love, eluding undesirable suitors and avoiding family scandals which would almost certainly ruin any hope of a financially advantageous marriage for you or any of your sisters.

VOLUME ONE

The news that nearby Netherfield Park has been let to a man of above five thousand pounds a year greatly pleases your mother, who is utterly convinced that this will immediately enhance the prospects of one or another of her daughters marrying well. You learn from your neighbours Sir William and Lady Lucas that Mr Bingley is quite young, wonderfully handsome, extremely agreeable and, to crown the whole, he means to be at the next assembly with a large party – nothing could be more delightful! To be fond of dancing is a certain step towards falling in love; and your mother entertains very lively hopes of one of you attaining Mr Bingley's heart.

When his party enters the assembly room it consists of only five altogether – Mr Bingley, his two sisters, the husband of the eldest, and another young man. Mr Bingley is good-looking and gentlemanlike; he has a pleasant countenance and easy, unaffected manners. His sisters are fine women, with an air of decided fashion; his brother-in-law, Mr Hurst, looks the gentleman but lacks the manners and grace of one; whereas his friend Mr Darcy soon draws the attention of the room by his fine, tall person, handsome features, noble mien and the report, which is in general circulation within five minutes after his entrance, of his having ten thousand a year. The gentlemen pronounce him to be a fine figure of a man, the ladies declare he is much handsomer than Mr Bingley, and he is looked at with great admiration for about half the evening, till his manners give a disgust which turns the tide of his popularity.

He is discovered to be proud, to be above his company and above being pleased; and not all his large estate in Derbyshire can save him from having a most forbidding, disagreeable countenance, and being unworthy of comparison with his friend.

Your own opinion of him is soon decided when, having been obliged by the scarcity of gentlemen to sit down for two dances, you are near enough to overhear a conversation between him and Mr Bingley in which Mr Bingley draws Darcy's attention to the fact that you are without a partner. Mr Darcy turns to look at you for a moment till, catching your eye, he withdraws his own and coldly says, 'She is tolerable, but not handsome enough to tempt me; and I am in no humour at present to give consequence to young ladies who are slighted by other men.'

This leaves you with far from cordial feelings towards Darcy. You soon recover yourself, however, and at your first opportunity you tell your story with great spirit among your friends and family.

When you all return home to reflect on the evening, it becomes apparent that, based on Mr Bingley's having danced with Jane as many as two times through the course of the evening, your mother has high hopes of his shortly becoming her own son-in-law.

A few days later, you and Jane wait on the ladies of Netherfield Park, and the visit is returned in due form. You cannot like them, though their kindness to Jane, such as it is, has some value in it, since it arises in all probability from the influence of their brother's admiration. That he does admire her you are certain; and to you it is equally evident that Jane is on the way to being very much in love, though, because of her great composure, it is not likely to be discovered by the rest of the world.

A few days later, Jane receives a dinner invitation from Miss Bingley and Mrs Hurst, but to your mother's disappointment it would seem that Mr Bingley is dining out on this particular evening. Your mother refuses to give Jane the carriage and insists on sending her on horseback, knowing very well that it is likely to rain and Jane will be forced to stay the night at Netherfield. You are well used to your mother's schemes by now, but endangering Jane's health solely for the purpose of promoting romance seems to you not only careless and unfeeling, but also hardly likely to achieve its end: a red nose and a sore throat have not often inspired feelings of ardour.

Not long after your sister's departure, your mother's scheme is rewarded by a heavy downpour of rain, but it is not until the following morning that she is aware of the full felicity of her contrivance. A note arrives from Jane stating that she has caught a bad cold, her friends will not hear of her leaving, and they are currently awaiting the arrival of the doctor. Your anxiety for your sister's welfare is so great that you desire to visit Netherfield to assess her condition. Your mother refuses to give you either horse or carriage despite the unpleasant conditions and you therefore embark on the three-mile walk to Netherfield alone.

You make your journey at a quick pace without a care for your appearance, eagerly jumping over stiles and springing over puddles, spurred on by your creditable devotion to your sister. You hastily climb over a gate and find yourself in a field you don't recognise. There are two paths ahead of you.

To take the path to the left, turn to page 12.

To take the path to the right, turn to page 22.

You stay a few days longer to ensure Jane is fully recovered. Your caution is justified as she takes a turn for the worse again that evening, and you are obliged to stay yet longer. Thankfully, the following day there is a change in company as a Mr Henry Crawford, his sister Mary and their friend Mr Yates arrive at Netherfield.

Mary Crawford is remarkably pretty, and Henry Crawford, though not handsome, has air, countenance and a fortune of five thousand pounds a year; and the manners of both are lively and pleasant. Mr Yates has not much to recommend him beyond his large estate of Mansfield Park, and a love of acting. He suggests that the Netherfield party put on a play and the Bingleys and Crawfords agree that it is a capital plan. Mr Bingley is a great admirer of the theatre, and is delighted to have the chance to try a little acting himself; Miss Bingley, it appears, is a great admirer of Mr Crawford, and is only too happy to join in his scheme; and Mrs Hurst refuses to be left out of anything Miss Bingley is doing. You are greatly surprised by their want of propriety; Mr Darcy protests, but in vain, and the play *Lovers' Vows* is decided upon. You are rather surprised that it has even been considered; the female characters are so unfit to be expressed by any woman of modesty that you can hardly suppose the Bingley sisters can be aware of what they are engaging in. You, at least, refuse to be drawn into such an improper scheme, but the happy actors realise they are missing a Cottager's Wife and suddenly petition you to take the role.

'Me!' you cry in alarm. 'Indeed you must excuse me. I could not act anything if you were to give me the world. No, indeed, I cannot act.'

'Phoo! Phoo!' replies Mrs Hurst. 'Do not be so shamefaced. Every allowance will be made for you. We do not expect perfection. You must get a brown gown, and a white apron, and a mob cap, and we must make you a few wrinkles, and a little of the crow's foot at the corner of your eyes, and you will be a very proper, little old woman.'

'You must excuse me,' you insist, thinking how insupportable it would be to act in a production with those for whom you have such low regard, 'indeed you must.'

'Do not urge her, madam,' interrupts Mr Darcy. 'It is not fair to urge her in this manner. You see she does not like to act. Let her choose for herself, as well as the rest of us. Do not urge her any more.'

You are quite taken by surprise at this show of gallantry from Mr Darcy, and know not what to make of it.

The role of Cottager's Wife is cut from the play, and rehearsals commence the next day. You watch with concern as Mr Crawford pays his attentions to Mrs Hurst. You are very glad that Jane is not present to witness Bingley's sister indulging in a flirtation. Perhaps fearing that his behaviour is giving rise to hopes that he has no intentions of fulfilling, however, on the third day of rehearsals Mr Crawford has an apparent change of heart and redirects his attention away from Mrs Hurst and towards you, endeavouring, it would seem, to make you fall in love with him. Your contempt for him only increases and you are determined not to be taken in by his charms.

Over the next fortnight, however, Mr Crawford pays you such gallant attention that you begin to feel that he might be in love with you after all. Astonishing though it is, it really seems to be true. There is something in his eyes when he speaks to you that seems to communicate something beyond his words and he presses your hand with such meaning that you cannot help but soften your resolve against him. You can hardly believe yourself. You fight against it as best you can, but Mr Crawford seems sincerely to love you and you cannot resist his affections forever. However disingenuous he was when he first paid his attentions to you it seems as if, almost against his better judgement, he has genuinely fallen in love with you and is now entirely serious in his intentions. He seems to understand that you value good sense above all else and each day modifies his behaviour so that it is so different from what it has been, so far improved, that when Jane is well enough to join you all downstairs once again, even *she* begins to wish you in love with him.

Your heart and mind are in tumult; you are wary of his fickle heart, but cannot remain immune to such devotion. At the end of his third week at Netherfield, Mr Crawford makes a formal declaration.

To give in to your overwhelming impulses and accept Mr Crawford, trusting in his change of character and the security of his five thousand a year, turn to page 47.

To refuse him, wary of his sudden change in character, turn to page 53.

'The Sensible Type'

You are all sense and no sensibility. Though greatly distressed, your emotions are not likely to be discovered by anybody: you conceal them so well you are barely sensible of them yourself. To increase your sensibility, try harder to give your family pain at every moment by refusing to eat, talk or come out of your room, until they are so concerned for your welfare that a doctor is called.

Continue on page 34.

After about half a mile you make a sudden turn into a path deeply shaded by elms on each side. You have advanced some way when you suddenly perceive at a small distance before you, a gang of ruffians. A child on the watch comes towards you to beg, causing you to let out a great scream. How they might have behaved had you been more courageous is doubtful, but such an invitation for attack cannot be resisted. You are soon assailed by half a dozen children, headed by a stout woman and a thickset boy. Growing more and more frightened, you promise them money and, taking out your purse, give them a shilling, begging them not to want more, or to use you ill.

You are then able to walk forwards, though slowly, and you move away from the group – but your fear and your purse are too tempting, and you are followed, or rather surrounded, by the whole gang, demanding more. When you confess that you have none, they set about attacking you until you are so badly hurt that even after your physical injuries have healed your disposition is forever changed to one of nervousness and distrust, causing you to keep to your room at all times and shun all company beyond that of your immediate family from this day forth.

THE END

Oh dear. You have failed to complete your mission.

For the chance to keep playing, return to page 6 and choose again.

Shortly after your return, your father announces that he is expecting an addition to your family party. About a month ago he received a letter from your cousin Mr Collins who, since your family estate is entailed away, may turn you all out of your house as soon as he pleases when your father is dead. Your mother cannot bear to hear that odious man's name mentioned, but is a little softened by some of what Mr Collins has to say.

He has been so fortunate as to be distinguished by the patronage of the Right Honourable Lady Catherine de Bourgh, widow of Sir Lewis de Bourgh, whose bounty and beneficence has preferred him to the valuable rectory of the parish of Hunsford in Kent. He begs leave to apologise for being next in the entail of Longbourn estate and being the means of injuring Mr Bennet's amiable daughters, and assures your father of his readiness to make those daughters all possible amends. You can only guess that he means by marrying one of you. Your father confesses to you great hopes of finding him ridiculous, and there is a mixture of servility and self-importance in his letter which promises well.

Mr Collins is punctual to his time and is received with great politeness by the whole family. He is a tall, heavy-looking young man of five-and-twenty. His air is grave and stately, and his manners are extremely formal. During dinner Mr Collins launches into a panegyric on his patroness Lady Catherine de Bourgh and her sickly daughter Anne, towards whom he conceives himself peculiarly bound to pay little attentions which he admits to often rehearsing.

It soon becomes clear that you were right: Mr Collins means to choose one of you for a wife to make amends for inheriting your father's estate. You sincerely hope he does not choose you as his means of doing so, but are no less concerned when you see that it is Jane's lovely face that quickly captures his attention. You mention it to your mother, who soon cautions him against her. Far from being disheartened, Mr Collins simply redirects his attentions towards you instead, seemingly without a second thought. You wish you had kept quiet.

The following morning you, your sisters and Mr Collins walk to Meryton to visit your aunt Philips. A small militia regiment has recently taken residence at Meryton, and your sisters are always keen to get the latest news on the officers from your obliging aunt. As you enter Meryton, your attention is soon caught by a young man of most gentlemanlike appearance walking on the other side of the way with Mr Denny, an officer with whom you have become acquainted at your aunt Philips's. Mr Denny entreats permission to introduce his friend, Mr Wickham, who has accepted a commission in Denny's corps. His appearance is greatly in his favour: he has all the best parts of beauty – a fine countenance, a good figure and very pleasing address. You are particularly happy your sisters suggested a walk this morning.

You are all standing and talking together very agreeably when the sound of horses draws your notice, and Darcy and Bingley come riding down the street directly towards you. They are just beginning the usual civilities when Mr Darcy's eyes are suddenly arrested by the sight of the stranger and, happening to see the countenance of both as they look at each other, you are all astonishment at the effect of the meeting. Both change colour, one looks white, the other red. Mr Wickham, after a few moments, touches his hat – a salutation which Mr Darcy just deigns to return. It is impossible to imagine what could be the meaning of it; it is impossible not to long to know.

In another minute Mr Bingley, without seeming to have noticed what has just passed, takes leave and rides on with his friend, while Mr Denny and Mr Wickham accompany you to the door of Mr Philips's house, and then make their bows.

You discuss Mr Wickham with your aunt, and she promises to invite him to a dinner she has planned for some of the other officers tomorrow night. The prospect of such delights is very cheering, and you part in mutual good spirits. As you walk home, you relate to Jane what you saw pass between Wickham and Darcy; but unfortunately Jane can no more explain such behaviour than you.

The following day, your coach conveys you all at a suitable hour to Meryton. When Mr Wickham walks into the room, you feel that he is far beyond the other officers in person, countenance, air and walk. He is the happy man towards whom almost every female eye turns, and you are the happy woman by whom he finally seats himself. The card tables are placed, and while the others play at whist, Mr Wickham talks to you. You are longing to ask the history of his acquaintance with Mr Darcy, but delicacy forbids you. Your curiosity is unexpectedly relieved, however, when Mr Wickham begins the subject himself, and after making sure that neither you nor anyone else in the neighbourhood feels any sentiment towards Mr Darcy beyond a general disgust at his pride, Wickham begins his account.

Wickham's reason for avoiding Darcy arises from a sense of very great ill-usage. To your astonishment you learn that, born in the same parish and within the same park, they passed the greatest part of their youth together. Wickham's father gave up everything to be of use to the late Mr Darcy, and devoted all his time to the care of the Darcy family property, Pemberley. He was highly esteemed by Mr Darcy as a most intimate, confidential friend, and immediately before Wickham's father died, the late Mr Darcy gave him a voluntary promise of providing for young Wickham. He bequeathed him the best Church living it was in his power to bestow; but you are horrified to learn that when the living next became available it was given elsewhere. You are appalled by what you hear, and your opinion of Darcy sinks lower and lower. According to Wickham, there was an informality in the terms of the bequest, and young Mr Darcy asserted that Wickham had forfeited all claim to it by extravagance and imprudence, though Wickham can accuse himself of having done nothing to deserve to lose it. You do not doubt him, and can hardly imagine it possible that one as affable and reasonable as Wickham could be accused of extravagance and imprudence. It is much easier to believe that Mr Darcy could have manipulated the informality of the bequest to suit his own ends.

Wickham believes that Darcy was jealous of the attention paid to Wickham by his father after the death of Wickham's own. You are shocked and disgusted, but you suddenly remember Darcy's boasting at Netherfield of the implacability of his resentments, of his having an unforgiving temper. Mr Wickham's account confirms all that you have long suspected concerning Darcy. From almost the first moment you saw him you knew him to be a proud, disagreeable man, and nothing that he has done since has had any effect beyond confirming this first impression. You wonder that Wickham can bear to remain in the same county as Mr Darcy.

'I hope,' you venture, 'your plans in favour of Hertfordshire will not be affected by his being in the neighbourhood.'

'Oh! No – it is not for *me* to be driven away by Mr Darcy. If *he* wishes to avoid seeing *me,* he must go.'

You are very pleased to hear it. You are again deep in thought, struggling to take in the full meaning of what you have heard, and after a time you exclaim, 'To treat in such a manner the godson, the friend, the favourite of his father! I wonder that the very pride of this Mr Darcy has not made him just to you!'

'It *is* wonderful,' replies Wickham, 'for almost all his actions may be traced to pride; and pride has often been his best friend.'

You are extremely surprised to hear Wickham defend the very man who has been the means of ruining his every prospect, and rather wonder that Mr Wickham should *commend* his excessive and offensive pride.

'Can such abominable pride as his have ever done him good?' you ask, doubtingly.

'His pride has often led him to be liberal and generous,' explains Wickham, 'to give his money freely, to display hospitality, to assist his tenants and relieve the poor. Family pride, and *filial* pride, for he is very proud of what his father was, have done this. He has also *brotherly* pride, which, with *some* brotherly affection, makes him a very kind and careful guardian of his sister.'

You find it hard to believe, and regard this favourable account of Darcy as proof merely of Mr Wickham's admirable generosity of character.

Miss Darcy he describes as 'too much like her brother – very, very proud'.

You are extremely pleased to have your opinion of Mr

— 19 —

Darcy confirmed by Mr Wickham, and it appears to you, indeed, that on almost everything the two of you discuss, your thoughts and opinions are as one. You cannot but smile when you think on it, and your attachment to Wickham increases with every pleasing reflection.

The next moment, Mr Wickham's attention is suddenly caught when he overhears Mr Collins talking of his patroness Lady Catherine de Bourgh. Wickham informs you that Lady Catherine and Darcy's mother, Lady Anne Darcy, are sisters; Lady Catherine's daughter Miss de Bourgh will have a very large fortune, and it is believed that she and her cousin Mr Darcy will unite the two estates. This information makes you smile, as you think of poor Miss Bingley. Vain indeed must be all her attentions to Darcy if he is already self-destined to another.

You go away that night with your head full of Mr Wickham and relate his story to Jane the next day. She listens with astonishment and concern; she cannot believe either of them to be in the wrong, and determines therefore to continue to think well of them both. You cannot agree with her on this point and can easily believe Mr Darcy to be in the wrong. You tease her for her inability to think ill of anyone, no matter how incriminating the evidence against them might be.

The two of you are summoned from your conversation by the arrival of some of the very persons of whom you have been speaking; Mr Bingley and his sisters have come to Longbourn to give their personal invitation for the long-expected ball at Netherfield.

Continue on page 40.

The path leads you to the top of the field, from where you can clearly see the way to Netherfield. You quicken your pace a little and arrive at the house with weary ankles, dirty stockings and a face glowing with the warmth of exercise. You feel alive and refreshed and are eager to see Jane. You are shown into the breakfast parlour, where all but Jane are assembled – and where your appearance creates a great deal of surprise. That you should have walked three miles, in such dirty weather, without a care for your state of dress, and by yourself, appears almost incredible to Miss Bingley and Mrs Hurst, and they clearly hold you in contempt for it. Mr Darcy says very little, and Mr Hurst nothing at all. You are sure Mr Darcy thinks ill of you for coming so far alone, but care not what he thinks. You care even less for Mr Hurst's opinion, and in any case, from his vacant expression it seems likely that he is probably thinking only of his breakfast.

You are taken to your sister immediately, and you are both delighted to see one another. The doctor has advised Jane that she must remain in bed to get the better of her violent cold, but you are relieved to see she is in no real danger and when the clock strikes three you feel you must return home. Miss Bingley offers you the use of the carriage but when Jane testifies concern over your parting, Miss Bingley is obliged to extend an invitation to remain at Netherfield for the present, which you accept. You earnestly hope Jane's illness will not be a long-lasting one.

At dinner that night the sisters enquire after Jane, repeat three or four times how much they are grieved, how shocking it is to have a bad cold, and how excessively they dislike being ill themselves; and then think no more of the matter. When dinner is over, you return directly to your sister and gladly pass the evening in her quiet company. When at last you have the comfort of seeing her asleep, your sense of propriety compels you to go downstairs and join your hosts, despite your inclinations to the contrary. Just as you are about to open the drawing-room door, you catch your name being used in a conversation between Miss Bingley and Mrs Hurst, and you pause outside for a moment, not wishing to cause any embarrassment by interrupting them. You cannot help overhearing what they have to say about you, and it gives you no very great pleasure. Your manners are pronounced to be very bad indeed, a mixture of pride and impertinence: you have no conversation, no style, no taste and no beauty. You cannot help but smart at such abuse of your character, but since you have no respect for their opinion, you do not take it to heart. Mr Bingley, at least, defends your character, and your affection for him can only grow as a result; you cannot blame him for his sisters. You take a moment to recover your composure, and when they have quite finished, you enter the room with renewed and vigorous feelings of antipathy towards Mr Bingley's sisters, and take a seat at the furthest possible distance from them.

The next day passes much as the day before, and in the evening you join the rest of the party in the drawing room. While Mrs Hurst sings with her sister you cannot help observing how frequently Mr Darcy's eyes are fixed on you. You are vexed by the impertinence of it. That he should look at you because he dislikes you is very strange indeed, and yet you hardly know how to suppose that you could be an object of admiration to so great a man. What can he mean by it? You decide, at last, that you draw his notice because there is something about you more wrong and reprehensible, according to his ideas of right, than in any other person present. The supposition does not pain you, however; you like him too little to care for his approbation.

After playing some Italian songs on the pianoforte, Miss Bingley varies the charm by playing a lively Scotch air; and soon afterwards Mr Darcy, drawing near you, says to you, 'Do not you feel a great inclination, Miss Bennet, to seize such an opportunity of dancing a reel?'

You smile, but make no answer. If he wants to insult you he may, but you will not give him the satisfaction of rising to such an inducement. He repeats the question, with some surprise at your silence and, really annoyed by him this time, you reply with affected gaiety, 'Oh! I heard you before; but I cannot immediately determine what to say in reply. You wanted me, I know, to say "Yes", that you might have the pleasure of despising my taste; but I always delight in overthrowing those kind of schemes, and cheating a person of their premeditated contempt. I have therefore made up my mind to tell you that I do not want to dance a reel at all – and now despise me if you dare.'

'Indeed I do not dare,' he replies.

Having rather expected to affront him, you are amazed at his gallantry and cannot readily find the words to form a response. You are saved the difficulty of the task, however, by Miss Bingley who, having seen enough to be jealous, quickly draws Mr Darcy's attention away, her great anxiety for Jane's recovery receiving considerable assistance from her renewed desire to get rid of you.

*J*ane is soon so much recovered that she is able to leave her room for a few hours in the evening. You are anxious to return home but are unsure whether Jane is well enough recovered for the journey. She appears to be in good health, but you know she would never admit to needing to stay longer if she felt it would be an inconvenience to anyone.

To trust in her improved appearance and urge Jane to borrow Mr Bingley's carriage immediately, turn to page 33.

To suggest Jane takes advantage of the restorative properties of fresh air and exercise by walking back the way you came, turn to page 29.

To stay a few days longer to ensure Jane is fully recovered, turn to page 7.

'The Sentimental Type'

You care not a jot for sense or reason, and let your heart govern all your decisions. A triumph of sensibility! Your family is in great pain witnessing your distress, and you make yourself so ill that at last a doctor is called.

Continue on page 34.

*Y*ou accept the Colonel's offer and you both return to Hertfordshire to be married at the earliest opportunity. You find yourself submitting to new attachments, entering on new duties, placed in a new home, a wife, mistress of a family and the patroness of a village. Your own happiness is perhaps surpassed only by Colonel Brandon's, and your mother, always having preferred Jane to you, is for once inclined to think you her favourite for being the first of her daughters to marry, and for marrying so well.

THE END

Congratulations. You have successfully completed your mission.

*Y*ou set off early the next morning and deliver Jane safely to the garden gate. You are enjoying the freedom of a walk in the open air so much that you decide to go on alone. You continue past your house and gaily ascend the hills before you, catching in your face the animating gales of a high south-westerly wind. Suddenly the clouds unite over your head, and a driving rain sets full in your face. You turn back, running with all possible speed down the steep side of the hill, which leads immediately to your garden gate, but a false step brings you suddenly to the ground. A gentleman carrying a gun happens to be passing up the hill and within a few yards of you when your accident happens, and runs to your assistance. Your foot has been twisted in the fall and you are scarcely able to stand. The gentleman offers his services, and perceiving that your modesty declines what your situation renders necessary, takes you up in his arms without further delay and carries you down the hill. He bears you directly into the house and quits not his hold till he has seated you in a chair in the parlour. Your mother and sisters rise up in amazement at your entrance, and the eyes of all are fixed on him with an evident wonder and, you are sure, a secret admiration. He apologises for his intrusion by relating its cause in a manner so frank and so graceful that his person, which is uncommonly handsome, receives additional charms from his voice and expression. Your mother thanks him again and again and invites him to be seated, but this he declines for fear of leaving a water mark. She then begs to know to whom she is obliged. His name, he replies, is Willoughby, his estate Combe Magna in Somersetshire and his present home is at Meryton with his cousin Mrs Smith, from whence he hopes your mother will allow him the honour of calling tomorrow to enquire after you. The honour is readily granted, and he then departs, to make himself still more interesting, in the midst of a heavy rain, with no regard for what havoc it might wreak on his health – or his coat. Your mother declares him more handsome even than Mr Bingley, and her rapturous delight at making his acquaintance is surpassed only by your own.

You earnestly hope that Willoughby will honour his promise to visit you in the morning and you are not disappointed: early the next day he calls to enquire after your health. You receive him with great pleasure and he converses with you for many hours. You feel as if you have known each other for a lifetime; his fondness for Cowper's poetry is second only to his love of Shakespeare's sonnets in the innumerable list of his merits. As your ankle's swelling subsides your affection grows, and soon your quiet neighbourhood is disturbed by your riotous and imprudent jaunts in his carriage. Love has robbed you of your characteristic good sense and, unable to see or think of the world beyond your intimate sphere of two, you throw caution and prudence to the wind. Jane cautions you against such unrestrained behaviour but you are so very much in love that you disregard her advice, believing that where the heart leads, no wrong can follow. Willoughby begs a lock of hair from you and, taking up your scissors, cuts off a long one, kisses it, folds it up in a piece of white paper and puts it into his pocketbook.

You and your family are certain that it will not be long until the two of you are united in marriage, and one Sunday you stay behind from church to facilitate the anticipated proposal. No sooner have your mother and sisters entered the house on their return, however, than you come out of the parlour with your handkerchief at your eyes, and without looking at them, run up the stairs. Willoughby has just told you that Mrs Smith has exercised the privilege of riches upon a poor dependent cousin by sending him on business to London. He has no intention of returning to Meryton.

This latest disappointment will be a great test of your sensibility. Your reaction must exactly match the level of your distress. Take the following Sensibility Test and see which Sensibility Type you are.

The man you love, and from whom you were expecting a proposal of marriage, suddenly leaves the countryside with no immediate plans to return.

Do you:

a) Try your hardest to conceal your emotions from your family for fear of giving them any share of the pain that you feel all too strongly yourself.

b) Take your place at dinner that night with eyes red and swollen, restraining your tears with difficulty, neither eating nor speaking, but awake the next morning with a greater degree of composure following a reasonable night's sleep.

c) Take your place at dinner that night with eyes red and swollen, restraining your tears with difficulty, neither eating nor speaking, then rise from your bed the next morning more in need of repose than when you lay down in it, unable to talk, unwilling to take any nourishment and giving pain every moment to your family.

If you answered a), turn to page 11.

If you answered b), turn to page 55.

If you answered c), turn to page 27.

*Y*ou urge Jane to borrow Mr Bingley's carriage immediately and the communication excites so many professions of concern for Jane that your going is deferred till the morrow. To Mr Darcy you imagine your departure is welcome intelligence; he scarcely speaks ten words to you through the whole of Saturday, and though you are at one time left by yourselves for half an hour, he adheres most conscientiously to his book, and will not even look at you. On Sunday you take leave of the whole party in the liveliest spirits.

Proceed to page 14.

*F*ollowing Willoughby's removal from Hertfordshire, your melancholy and your family's concern continue uninterrupted until you are invited to London by your friend Charlotte's parents, Sir William and Lady Lucas. Though it must mean being away from Mr Bingley at this important stage of their courtship, Jane generously agrees to accompany you. The prospect of seeing Willoughby again brightens your spirits immeasurably, and you feel that all will soon be put to rights.

Your departure takes place in the first week in January and you arrive three days later, glad to be released, after such a journey, from the confinement of a carriage, and ready to enjoy all the luxury of a good fire. As dinner is not to be ready in less than two hours from your arrival, you determine to employ the interval in writing to Willoughby.

You can scarcely eat any dinner, and when you afterwards return to the drawing room you anxiously listen to the sound of every carriage. A loud rap is suddenly heard which cannot be mistaken for one at any other house and, expecting Willoughby, you start up and move towards the door. Everything is silent, and the suspense is overwhelming. It is to your great disappointment, then, that Sir William's friend Colonel Brandon appears. The Colonel has become a friend to you and Jane on his frequent visits to Sir William back in Longbourn and has long since been a great admirer of yours. His face is not unpleasing and, though he is on the wrong side of five-and-thirty, his countenance is sensible and his address is particularly gentlemanlike. You acknowledge him to be a good man, but you feel nothing above common regard for him and since you cannot return them, his attentions are therefore not altogether welcome.

About a week after your arrival you find Willoughby's card on the table when you come in from the morning's drive. Your heart leaps, and you are dearly disappointed that you missed him. You insist on being left behind the next morning when the others go out, but Willoughby does not return.

The following day you learn from Jane that Colonel Brandon has visited. She tells you that he had asked her, in a voice of some agitation, when he was to congratulate her on the acquisition of a brother. It seems that others have been talking of your engagement to Willoughby as a certainty. This only increases your feeling of distress: you alone know that no formal engagement has been entered into. From what she tells you, it seems that Jane led Colonel Brandon to believe that you and Willoughby *are* engaged, and though she does not press you, you know that she is waiting for confirmation from you as to whether or not it is true. You remain silent, however, reluctant to admit that you are not, and still clinging to the hope that you will very soon be so. Jane finishes by relating to you with concern Colonel Brandon's parting words: 'To your sister I wish all imaginable happiness; to Willoughby that he may endeavour to deserve her.'

'What do you think he could have meant by it?' Jane asks with evident concern.

She is worried that the Colonel might know something about Willoughby's character that has been hidden from you, but you pay no attention to her concerns. It seems to you only the natural sentiment of a man disappointed in love, and you immediately turn your thoughts back to Willoughby, and your anxiety over when he will come to you.

During the next four days Willoughby neither comes nor writes.

You are engaged to attend Lady Lucas to a party, for which, wholly dispirited, careless of your appearance, and seeming equally indifferent whether you go or stay, you prepare without one look of hope or one expression of pleasure.

You arrive in due time at the place of destination, and when you have paid your tribute of politeness by curtsying to the lady of the house, you are permitted to mingle in the crowd. You sit down close to the card table but do not remain in this manner long before you perceive Willoughby standing within a few yards of you, in earnest conversation with a very fashionable-looking young woman. With a countenance glowing with sudden delight, you go to move towards him but Jane instantly catches hold of you.

'Why does he not look at me?' you whisper to Jane, your anxiety growing with every passing moment.

'Pray, be composed,' urges Jane. 'Perhaps he has not observed you yet.'

This, however, you know is more than she can believe herself. Such trying circumstances rob you of your reason, and you cannot calm your agitated nerves however hard you try. You sit down at last, but your impatience affects every feature.

At last he turns round again, and regards you both; you start up, and hold out your hand to him. He approaches, and addressing himself rather to Jane than you, as if wishing to avoid your eye and determined not to observe your attitude, enquires in a hurried manner after your mother and asks how long you have been in town. His cold civility is so cruel a shock that you do not immediately know what to say in reply. Your face crimsons over, and you exclaim in a voice of the greatest emotion, 'Good God! Willoughby, what is the meaning of this? Have you not received my letters? Will you not shake hands with me?'

He cannot then avoid the act, but your touch seems painful to him, and he holds your hand only for a moment. You try everything in your power to contain your distress and Willoughby too appears to be struggling for composure. After a moment's pause, he speaks with calmness.

'I did myself the honour of calling in Berkeley Street last Tuesday, and very much regretted that I was not fortunate enough to find yourselves and Lady Lucas at home. My card was not lost, I hope.'

A thousand feelings rush upon you at once and, try as you might, you cannot hide your suffering.

'But have you not received my notes?' you cry, before taking hold of yourself and continuing in a lower voice. 'Here is some mistake, I am sure – some dreadful mistake. What can be the meaning of it? Tell me, Willoughby, what is the matter?'

He makes no reply; his complexion changes and all his embarrassment returns; but as if, on catching the eye of the young lady with whom he had been previously talking, he feels the necessity of instant exertion, he recovers himself again and after saying, 'Yes, I had the pleasure of receiving the information of your arrival in town, which you were so good as to send me', turns hastily away with a slight bow and joins his friend.

Never could you have imagined that one once so passionate could be so unfeeling towards you, and your wretchedness is beyond measure. Shock, above all else, overwhelms you. Looking dreadfully white you sink into your chair, and Jane, expecting every moment to see you faint, tries to screen you from the observation of others, for which you are grateful. In a short time Jane sees Willoughby quit the room by the door towards the staircase, and telling you that he is gone, urges the impossibility of speaking to him again that evening as a fresh argument for you to be calm. You are too miserable to stay a minute longer and instantly beg Jane to entreat Lady Lucas to take you home.

*B*efore the housemaid has lit your fire the next day, you write to Willoughby by what little light your window affords. As breakfast is a favourite meal with Lady Lucas, it lasts a considerable time, and all the while you think of Willoughby. Just as you finish eating, a letter in a familiar hand is delivered to you which you eagerly catch from the servant.

Proceed to page 48.

$\mathcal{T}$ill you enter the drawing room at Netherfield and look in vain for Mr Wickham among the cluster of red coats there assembled, a doubt of his being present never occurs to you. Mr Denny tells you that Wickham has been obliged to go to town on business and is not yet returned, adding, with a significant smile, 'I do not imagine his business would have called him away just now, if he had not wished to avoid a certain gentleman here.'

Every feeling of displeasure against Darcy that this summons in you is sharpened by immediate disappointment. You are in conversation with Charlotte Lucas, when you find yourself suddenly addressed by Mr Darcy, who takes you so much by surprise in his application for your hand that you are at a loss for some moments as to what to say. You are in such a shock that, without knowing what you do, you accept him. He walks away again immediately to join the other dancers as they prepare to begin, and you are left to fret over your own want of presence of mind.

You take your place in the set, and read in your neighbours' looks their amazement in beholding you standing opposite Mr Darcy. That the man who had not thought you handsome enough to dance with when you first met should now actively seek you out is surprising indeed, and you know not how to account for it. Though you dislike Darcy, you cannot deny that it is a most unexpected honour to be asked to dance with him.

You both dance for some time without speaking a word. After a while, you make some slight observation on the dance; he replies, and is again silent. You are determined to make him speak, however, and will not give up. After a pause of some minutes, you address him a second time with, 'It is your turn to say something now, Mr Darcy. I talked about the dance, and you ought to make some kind of remark on the size of the room, or the number of couples.'

He smiles.

'Do you talk by rule then, while you are dancing?' he asks.

He means to insult you but is unsuccessful. Instead you are amused by his attempt, and choose to retaliate not by denying, but conceding the point.

'Sometimes,' you reply with a smile. 'One must speak a little, you know. It would look odd to be entirely silent for half an hour together, and yet for the advantage of some, conversation ought to be so arranged as that they may have the trouble of saying as little as possible.'

From his change in expression, you see that the real meaning of your last comment is not lost upon him. You are silent till you have gone down the dance, when he asks you if you and your sisters do not very often walk to Meryton. You answer in the affirmative. You are pleased that he has provided you with the opportunity to broach the subject of Mr Wickham, as you are extremely curious to hear what he has to say on the matter. Unable to resist the temptation, you add shortly afterwards, 'When you met us there the other day, we had just been forming a new acquaintance.'

The effect is immediate. A deeper shade of hauteur overspreads his features, but he says not a word.

At length Darcy speaks, and in a constrained manner says, 'Mr Wickham is blessed with such happy manners as may ensure his making friends – whether he may be equally capable of retaining them, is less certain.'

At that moment Sir William Lucas appears and on perceiving Mr Darcy, stops with a bow of superior courtesy to compliment him on his dancing and his partner.

'I must hope to have this pleasure often repeated,' says Sir William, 'especially when a certain desirable event, my dear Miss Eliza,' he glances at your sister and Bingley, 'shall take place. What congratulations will then flow in! I appeal to Mr Darcy – but let me not interrupt you, sir.'

Sir William's allusion to his friend seems to strike Mr Darcy forcibly and his eyes are directed with a very serious expression towards Bingley and Jane. You feel keenly all the indiscretion of Sir William's so openly alluding to the general expectation of an imminent engagement being formed between Bingley and Jane, and grieve that Darcy should have been the one to hear it. You only hope, for Jane's sake, that whatever Darcy feels on the matter, Sir William's sentiments will not offend Bingley himself should he hear of them. You say no more, and when the dance is over you part in silence, dissatisfied and angry at Darcy's obstinate silence on the subject of Wickham. To you, it merely betrays his guilt in the matter.

You then seek Jane, who meets you with a smile of

such sweet complacency, a glow of such happy expression, as sufficiently marks how well she is satisfied with the evening's developments. You listen with delight to the happy, though modest, hopes which she entertains of Bingley's regard, and say all in your power to heighten her confidence in it.

When you sit down to supper shortly afterwards, however, you are deeply vexed to find that your mother is talking to Lady Lucas freely, openly, and of nothing else but of her expectation that Jane should be soon married to Mr Bingley. In vain do you endeavour to check the rapidity of your mother's words, for you perceive that they were overheard by Mr Darcy. The expression of his face changes gradually from indignant contempt to a composed and steady gravity. You blush and blush again with shame and vexation.

When supper is over, singing is talked of, and you have the mortification of seeing your plain younger sister Mary, after very little entreaty, preparing to oblige the company with a song. Mary's powers are by no means fitted for such a display; her voice is weak, and her manner affected. You are in agonies. You look at Bingley's sisters, and see them making signs of derision at each other, and at Darcy, who continues to look impenetrably grave. You catch your father's eye in an attempt to entreat his interference, lest Mary should be singing all night. He takes the hint, and when Mary has finished her second song, says aloud, 'That will do extremely well, child. You have delighted us long enough. Let the other young ladies have time to exhibit.'

Mary, though pretending not to hear, is somewhat disconcerted, and you are very sorry for your father's insensitive speech. To you it appears that had your family made an agreement to expose themselves as much as they could during the evening, it would have been impossible for them to play their parts with more spirit, or finer success.

At length you arise to take leave, your mother invites the whole family to Longbourn and Bingley readily engages to wait on her after his return from London, whither, you learn, he is obliged to go tomorrow for a short time. You return home, and take to your bed, very glad indeed that the evening and its miseries are over at last.

The next morning you are sitting with your mother and Kitty when Mr Collins enters and addresses Mrs Bennet directly.

'May I hope, madam, for your interest with your fair daughter Elizabeth, when I solicit for the honour of a private audience with her in the course of this morning?'

Before you have time for anything but a blush of surprise your mother instantly answers—

'Oh dear! Yes, certainly. I am sure Lizzy will be very happy – I am sure she can have no objection. Come, Kitty, I want you upstairs.'

As she is hastening away you call out in distress—

'Dear ma'am, do not go. I beg you will not go. Mr

Collins must excuse me. He can have nothing to say to me that anybody need not hear. I am going away myself.'

'No, no, nonsense, Lizzy. I desire you will stay where you are.' And upon seeing you really, with vexed and embarrassed looks, about to escape, she adds, 'Lizzy, I *insist* upon your staying and hearing Mr Collins.'

You cannot oppose such an injunction, and realising that it would be wisest to get it over as soon and as quietly as possible, you sit down again and try to conceal, by incessant employment, the feelings which are divided between distress and diversion. Mrs Bennet and Kitty walk off, and as soon as they are gone, Mr Collins begins—

'Almost as soon as I entered the house,' says he, 'I singled you out as the companion of my future life. But before I am run away with by my feelings on this subject, perhaps it will be advisable for me to state my reasons for marrying.'

The idea of Mr Collins, with all his solemn composure, being run away with by his feelings makes you so near laughing that you are unable to use the short pause he takes to try to stop him from going any further. He continues, therefore, by explaining that his reasons for marrying are pragmatic – 'it is a right thing for every clergyman in easy circumstances to set the example of matrimony in his parish' – and since he is to inherit your father's estate, he feels it is only right to ask you. In addition to these powerful incentives, his esteemed patroness has instructed him to do so, and he goes on to speak at great length about her, before remembering the job at hand and finishing with a flourish by assuring you of 'the violence of his affection'.

―∽

Mr Collins is making you a proposal.

To save your sisters and mother from being turned out of Longbourn after the unhappy but inevitable event of your father's death, turn to page 56 to accept Mr Collins. Your situation is critical.

To reject his offer, confident in your conviction that anything is to be preferred or endured rather than marrying without affection, turn to page 62.

You accept Mr Crawford and are wed soon afterwards. You have not been married long, however, before he elopes with Mrs Hurst, breaking your heart and involving you in a most terrible scandal. This ruins the chances of any of your sisters marrying well and you are all forced to work as governesses.

THE END

You have, regrettably, failed to complete your mission.

$\mathcal{R}$eading its contents you are shocked to the core. You feel yourself turning pale and growing faint, and you instantly run out of the room. Jane quickly follows you and finds you stretched on the bed, overcome by tears of grief, the most recent letter in your hand, and others lying by you. Though unable to speak, you put all the letters into Jane's hands and she reads the most recent first. He is sorry, she reads, if there was anything in his behaviour last night that did not meet your approbation; and is at a loss to discover in what point he could be so unfortunate as to offend you. His esteem for your whole family is very sincere, but if he has given rise to a belief of more than he felt, or meant to express, he shall reproach himself for not having been more guarded in his professions of that esteem. He finishes his letter by informing you that he is engaged to be married to another, and obeys your commands by returning all your letters, and the lock of hair which you 'so obligingly bestowed' on him.

Jane then reads the other letters you have written to Willoughby since arriving in London. Her condemnation of him does not blind her to the impropriety of their having been written at all, full as they are of such affection and confidence. It is an impropriety you are well aware of.

'I felt myself,' you argue in your defence, 'to be as solemnly engaged to him, as if the strictest legal covenant had bound us to each other.'

You long to go home, but are obliged to stay in London and fulfil your engagement with Lady Lucas. Two weeks after receiving Willoughby's letter you hear the news that he is married. Though you knew it must happen, you had until this moment held out hope that Willoughby would somehow yet be yours.

Your impatience to be gone increases every day. Fortunately, Lady Lucas is to visit her niece at Cleveland about the end of March for the Easter holidays and you receive a very warm invitation from her to go too. This must take you into the very county where you had once looked forward to going, but which you now dread seeing, the county where Willoughby lives, but you have little choice: though it is some distance out of your way, Lady Lucas has offered you her carriage to take you home afterwards and *that* is an offer you can't refuse. Jane too is eager to return home, and though she will never admit it, you are sure that a desire to be once more in the company of Mr Bingley is her chief inducement.

Your journey to Cleveland is safely performed and after three days' drive you enter the house with nerves greatly agitated from the consciousness of being not thirty miles from Combe Magna. Two sombre twilight walks on the third and fourth evenings of your being there in the most distant parts of the grounds, where the grass is the longest and wettest – assisted by the still greater imprudence of sitting in your wet shoes and stockings – give you an extremely violent cold.

The doctor is sent for, who pronounces your disorder to have a putrid tendency. Lady Lucas determines very early in the seizure that you will never get over it, and Colonel Brandon, recently arrived from London with Sir William, cannot expel from his mind the persuasion that he shall see you no more. Your repose becomes more and more disturbed; Jane perceives with alarm that you are not quite yourself; your pulse is lower and quicker than ever; and you talk so wildly of 'Papa' that Colonel Brandon offers to fetch him and departs immediately.

You remain in a heavy stupor for a number of days and are therefore unaware of the extraordinary event that happens during that time. It is not until you are sufficiently recovered, and your father and Colonel Brandon are safely arrived, that Jane decides to tell you the following story.

On the fourth day of your illness, the doctor had declared you entirely out of danger. On hearing a carriage drive up to the house Jane assumed it to herald the arrival of your father and the Colonel. She rushed towards the drawing room, entered it, and to her great surprise, saw only Willoughby. He had heard you were dying, and was greatly relieved therefore to hear that you were out of danger.

Immediately regretting having come, he then resolved to make it not a wasted journey by offering to Jane some explanation, some kind of apology for the past. Jane was unsure of how to react to such improper candidness, but felt at last that even Willoughby must be given a chance to defend himself, if such a thing were at all possible.

'He determined to pay his addresses to you,' says Jane, 'but, unwilling to enter into an engagement while his financial circumstances were so greatly embarrassed, put off the moment of doing so. Before he could confirm his affections to you, Mrs Smith was informed of a scandal involving Willoughby and an orphan in the care of Colonel Brandon by the name of Eliza.'

It was Sir William who was able to give Jane the full details of his friend Brandon's tragic story. Willoughby met, seduced and eloped with Eliza when she had just reached her fourteenth year and was staying at Bath with a friend. It was not until eight months later that Brandon could discover Eliza's whereabouts, by which time Willoughby had left her, never to return, in a situation of the utmost distress and heavy with child.

Willoughby's character – expensive, dissipated and worse than both – is now before you. A thousand feelings rush upon you at once. That you could have been so deceived in Willoughby is painful enough, but you have until this moment been unable to banish all your feelings of affection for him. This news, however, must kill them all.

'When Mrs Smith discovered this scandal,' Jane continues, 'Willoughby was dismissed from her favour and went to London with a "heavy heart" and thinking only of you. The unfeeling letter you received from him the day following the ball where you met was in fact composed by Miss Grey, whose fortune was the only thing that attracted Willoughby to her. In his own words, Lizzy, he "sacrificed his *and* your feelings to vanity and avarice to avoid a comparative poverty, which your affection and society would have deprived of all its horrors". By raising himself to affluence he lost everything that could make it a blessing.'

It is some time before you can fully recover from this story, though you betray nothing of your discomposure to Jane. Though you know it shouldn't be, it is of some comfort to know that Willoughby still loves you. It is hard for you to forget the Willoughby you knew in Hertfordshire, but for his dishonourable and disgraceful behaviour towards Eliza, you can never forgive him.

Over the next few days, your teasing father leads you to believe that Colonel Brandon has confessed his love for you. In the light of Jane's story, your feelings towards him are not as hard as they once were, and over time you come to think of him with some degree of fondness. After diligently reading you Shakespeare's sonnets through the long weeks of your recovery, Colonel Brandon makes you an offer of marriage.

If you wish to accept the kind, loving and wealthy colonel, turn to page 28.

If on the other hand, you feel that there might be a better match for you out there, you can refuse his offer and continue your search on page 61.

*Y*ou politely refuse Mr Crawford, but though you doubted him, it turns out that he has truly fallen in love with you. Unwilling to admit defeat readily, he secretly visits your father, and you are first made aware of this by the prompt arrival of your mother at Netherfield. Almost without introduction, she begins her abuse.

'You are a foolish, headstrong girl, Lizzy! The advantage or disadvantage of your family, of your parents, your sisters, never seems to have had a moment's share in your thoughts. How *they* might be benefited, how *they* must rejoice in such an establishment for you, is nothing to *you*. Oh, no! You think only of yourself, and because you do not feel for Mr Crawford exactly what a young heated fancy imagines to be necessary for happiness, you resolve to refuse him at once, and are, in a wild fit of folly, throwing away from you such an opportunity of being settled in life as will probably never occur to you again!'

You feel the blood rising in your cheeks. Though you acknowledge the truth of what she says about your obligation to your family, her abuse of your character does not please you. Far from acting in a 'wild fit of folly', you have given it your deepest consideration.

'I am sorry to give you pain, Mama,' you reply with as much composure as possible, 'but nothing you could say would induce me to accept a man I do not love. Mr Crawford's affections have but lately been directed towards me, and I am sure he will soon learn to redirect them towards another without material difficulty and will not therefore suffer too greatly from his present loss.'

Your mother takes leave of you in an agitation even angrier than the one in which she arrived.

Though he really loved you, Mr Crawford is not one given to reflection and does not pine for you long. He leaves Netherfield for London and it is not long before you hear a scandalous report of him: Mr Crawford has seduced and eloped with a married woman of society and is living with her in sin and shame, outcast from his family and all polite society. You are glad you refused him, and return home with Jane, leaving the Bingleys to recover from their friend's scandal.

Proceed to page 14.

'The Sense-ibility Type'

You have some sensibility, but a little too much sense for your own good. To be capable of sleep after such a shock makes Jane question whether you ever really loved Willoughby. To increase your sensibility, try to give a little more pain to your family by failing to sleep well, refusing to talk or take nourishment, and making your features as pallid as possible.

Continue on page 34.

To prevent him continuing his odious proposal one minute longer you hastily interject and accept his offer. His delight is great, and he professes himself to be the happiest man alive.

'Lady Catherine will, I'm sure, find you as delightful as I; have no fear on that point my dear Elizabeth!'

Mrs Bennet bursts into the room to offer her congratulations, and following her come Mary, Kitty and Lydia. You leave them to the attentions of Mr Collins, and go in search of Jane. Her shock at your news is great, which only pains you further. After she has had some moments to recover, she begins to see all the benefits of the situation, and encourages you to do the same.

'You have saved your sisters and mother, Lizzy,' says she. 'Think how grateful your whole family will be. You shall have all the pleasure of passing your adult years in familiar surroundings, with all your fondest recollections of the past to cheer you, and within an easy distance of your oldest friends and family. And Hunsford, I'm sure, will have much to recommend it in the meantime.'

You listen in silence, looking out of the window. She is trying to comfort you, but Jane's representation of your future seems bleak to you; it seems but a future spent thinking of the past. You survey the view and consider what a price has been paid to keep Longbourn within the family.

In the early afternoon your father calls you to his library.

'My dearest Lizzy,' says your father, 'pray comfort me. A most horrible joke has been played upon you. Your mother and sisters would have me believe that you are to be married to our cousin Mr Collins. Had it not been for Mr Collins's venturing so far as to apologise for the inconvenience that removing you from your family home might cause, I would not have wasted your time by calling you here. All this can be settled in a moment: tell me that you are not to marry Mr Collins.'

Your father's certainty that it cannot be true only serves to increase your discomfort.

'Father, I cannot. Mr Collins has proposed to me, and I have accepted him.'

Mr Bennet is silent. His face colours to a deep crimson, and then to the palest white. With a grave expression he finally speaks these words to you: 'I offer you my deepest sympathy. To this I will only add my advice: that your greatest chance of happiness lies in creating for yourself a library as soon as is possible after your arrival at Hunsford.'

You can only nod in reply.

'Very well, Lizzy, you may go.'

You leave the library in even heavier spirits than those in which you entered it.

Your wedding is a mercifully modest and quiet affair, with only your nearest friends and relatives present to witness the sealing of your unhappy fate. With many tears on your mother's side, and not a few on your own, your family sees you off in your carriage on the way to Hunsford, and certain wretchedness. You arrive at the parsonage in good time, and make the most of the remaining light by taking a walk in the garden you are to call yours until the unhappy day your father dies. You catch a glimpse of Rosings Park between the trees and wonder how many painful hours will be passed there in the ensuing months.

Time passes slowly. You write frequently to Charlotte and your family, but their replies are not as swift as you would have hoped. You are at pains to find enough employment to fill your days, and you take longer and longer walks so as to be spared the torment of conversation with your husband. You wonder how long you can continue in the present situation. You return home from your walks to a barrage of mindless talk from your husband. To call it conversation would be to do a disservice to the talents of Mr Collins, who is able to talk so ceaselessly without the need of an interlocutor as to render the term 'conversation' redundant. In vain do you seek a corner of the house in which he is out of hearing; no matter where you hide, he finds you.

And so it goes on, day after day, until you can bear it no longer. Having rejected all thoughts of suicide, you consider rendering yourself deaf to be your greatest chance of comfort. One day, when Mr Collins is spending the morning at Rosings consulting Lady Catherine over some proposed alterations to your garden path, you go to his room in search of a medical text that will explain how to perform this miracle. In increasing distress do you tear volume upon volume from the shelf in search of one that might give some hint as to how this injury might best be effected without incurring any further damage to your faculties. The time approaches when your husband must surely return, and still you have found nothing. With a cry of desperate panic do you greet the sound of Lady Catherine's carriage delivering him home. In a matter of moments the sound of his feet will be heard approaching you through the hall, shortly to be followed by the intolerable, unbearable, insufferable, torturous blabberings of the man himself. You tear at the pages of the volume in your hand, distracted and unhinged in your inexorable suffering. Before you know it his hand is on the door handle.

'My dearest Elizabeth, once again Lady Catherine has honoured us with her condescension and has suggested that we move the garden path seven degrees to the . . .'

He thrusts open the door just in time to see you, *Fordyce's Sermons* in hand and raised aloft, high above your head.

'My dear Elizabeth!'

'No more!' you cry, and with that you hurl *Fordyce's Sermons* directly at his head, killing him in an instant.

It is some moments before you regain your composure and come to a full realisation of the events that have just passed. Swiftly following on from your immediate feelings of guilt and horror comes the pleasant realisation that you are now free to return to Longbourn, and since there is no male heir left to whom the estate can be entailed away, you can only assume that it will remain with your own dear family. You wonder why you didn't think of it before, and begin to devise a way of making his death appear natural.

THE END

Delighted though you are, this marriage was clearly not for love, and your crime of passion, though understandable, would undeniably bring ruinous scandal upon your family were it ever to be discovered.

You have failed to complete your mission.

*D*ifficult though it is, you give up Colonel Brandon and return home to Longbourn with your father and Jane at the earliest opportunity. You never see the Colonel again and Sir William never speaks of him to you.

You turn your thoughts to Netherfield and hope that your extended absence has not harmed your sister's chances with Mr Bingley. You visit Netherfield the day following your return and find Mr Bingley as attentive to Jane as he ever was; Miss Bingley as unpleasant as she was wont to be; and Mr Darcy as taciturn and proud as you imagine he has been his entire life. You slip back into life at Longbourn with such ease that it soon feels as if you were never away.

Proceed to page 14.

'You are too hasty, sir,' you cry. 'You forget that I have made no answer. Let me do it without further loss of time. Accept my thanks for the compliment you are paying me, but it is impossible for me to do otherwise than decline.'

You feel an immediate sense of relief at having made your refusal, and having made it clearly. You go to leave the room, but to your great surprise, Mr Collins stops you by assuring you, with a formal wave of the hand, that he knows it is usual with young ladies to reject, at first, the addresses of the man whom they secretly mean to accept, and that he is therefore by no means discouraged by what you have just said, and hopes to lead you to the altar before long. You are astonished and vexed by his response. In vain do you endeavour to make him see that you would not dare to risk your happiness on the chance of being asked a second time; it seems that nothing you can say can induce him to take your refusal seriously. He seems unable to accept the idea that you could reject what he considers to be such an attractive offer.

'It does not appear to me that my hand is unworthy of your acceptance,' says he. 'You should take it into further consideration that in spite of your manifold attractions, it is by no means certain that another offer of marriage may ever be made you. Your portion is unhappily so small that it will in all likelihood undo the effects of your loveliness and other amiable qualifications.'

Your indignation at such an affront momentarily robs

you of words and you are therefore unable to interrupt him before he has finished saying that he has concluded that you are not serious in your rejection of him, and that he attributes it to your wish of increasing his love by suspense, 'according to the usual practice of elegant females'.

To such perseverance in wilful self-deception, you can make no reply. You immediately withdraw in silence before you do or say something you will regret.

When Mrs Bennet discovers that you have refused Mr Collins, she goes directly to your father and you are summoned to the library.

'Come here, child,' cries your father as you appear. 'I have sent for you on an affair of importance. I understand that Mr Collins has made you an offer of marriage which you have refused. Is it true?'

You reply that it is.

'Very well. We now come to the point. Your mother insists upon your accepting it. Is not it so, Mrs Bennet?'

'Yes, or I will never see her again.'

'An unhappy alternative is before you, Elizabeth. From this day you must be a stranger to one of your parents. Your mother will never see you again if you do *not* marry Mr Collins, and I will never see you again if you *do*.'

Your mother does not give up her point but coaxes and

threatens you by turns; Mr Collins is in a state of angry pride and barely speaks to you at all. A respite is afforded when Charlotte Lucas comes to spend the day with the family, and her civility in listening to Mr Collins is a seasonable relief to you all.

The following morning a letter is delivered to Jane from Netherfield. You see your sister's countenance change as she reads it and a glance from Jane invites you to follow her upstairs. The letter is from Caroline Bingley and the news is not what you had hoped: the whole party has left Netherfield, and are on their way to town – none of them to return to Hertfordshire this winter. Furthermore, Caroline praises Mr Darcy's sister Georgiana and expresses her hope that they will soon be sisters. Mr Bingley, she claims, admires Miss Darcy greatly already; and now that they are both in London, she believes it is just a matter of time before they are married. You, however, are not convinced, and treat the idea of Bingley never returning with the utmost contempt. You think that Miss Bingley sees that her brother is in love with Jane, *wants* him to marry Miss Darcy, and is doing her best therefore to separate Jane and Bingley. You cannot for a moment, however, suppose that those wishes, however openly or artfully spoken, could influence a young man as independent as Mr Bingley. You represent your feelings on the subject to Jane as forcibly as possible, and soon have the pleasure of seeing her hope restored.

*D*uring the chief of the following day, Charlotte is so kind as to listen to Mr Collins again, but her kindness extends further than you have any conception of. It would seem that the object of Charlotte's kindness was nothing else than to secure you from any return of Mr Collins's addresses, by engaging them towards herself. The following morning Charlotte calls after breakfast to inform you that Mr Collins has proposed to her and that she has accepted him. Your astonishment is so great as to overcome at first the bounds of decorum, and you cannot help crying out, 'Engaged to Mr Collins! My dear Charlotte, impossible!'

You rather hope, than believe, it to be impossible.

'Why should you be surprised, my dear Eliza? Do you think it incredible that Mr Collins should be able to procure any woman's good opinion, because he was not so happy as to succeed with you?'

To think of Charlotte throwing away her happiness on such a man as Mr Collins distresses you deeply, though you do your best to conceal the strength of your true feelings. Charlotte admits that Mr Collins is neither sensible nor agreeable; his society is irksome, and his attachment to her must be imaginary; but still he will be her husband. Without thinking highly either of men or of matrimony, she tells you, marriage has always been her object. You listen in silence, and are quite taken aback by her views. She argues that marriage is the only honourable provision for well-educated young women of small fortune, and however uncertain of giving happiness, must be their pleasantest preservative from want. This preservative she has now obtained; and at the age of twenty-seven, without having ever been handsome, she feels all the good luck of having ensured her future security. You can scarcely believe you are hearing your dearest childhood friend talking in this cold and calculated way, with no regard whatsoever for love. You feel as if you never knew her and are quite shaken.

'I am not romantic, you know,' she continues, 'I never was. I ask only a comfortable home; and considering Mr Collins's character, connections, and situation in life, I am convinced that my chance of happiness with him is as fair as most people can boast on entering the marriage state.'

'Undoubtedly,' you answer quietly; and after an awkward pause you return to the rest of the family.

Your disappointment in Charlotte makes you turn with fonder regard to your sister, for whose happiness you grow daily more anxious, as Bingley has now been gone a week and nothing has been heard of his return.

A letter from Miss Bingley eventually arrives, and puts an end to doubt. The very first sentence conveys the assurance of their being all settled in London for the winter and the rest praises Miss Darcy's manifold attractions once more. You are very disappointed to hear that Bingley will return no more, and while Jane accounts for it by believing that Bingley was never truly attached to her, *you* remain convinced his sisters and 'friend' have influenced him against her. You are very sorry for your sister, and this latest circumstance only fuels yet further your angry feelings towards Mr Darcy and Bingley's sisters.

Congratulations. You have completed Volume One.

Your choices have led you closer to marrying both prudently and for love.

Proceed to Volume Two on page 69.

VOLUME TWO

Mr Wickham's society is of material service in dispelling the gloom which the late perverse occurrences of Bingley's departure and Mr Collins's marriage plans have thrown on many of your family. You see Wickham often, and to his other recommendations is now added that of general unreserve. All that he has suffered from Mr Darcy is now openly acknowledged and publicly canvassed. Everybody is pleased to think how much they had always disliked Mr Darcy even before they had known anything of the matter. Wickham is a favourite throughout the neighbourhood, which only adds further charm to his attentions towards you.

On the following Monday, your mother has the pleasure of receiving her brother and his wife at Longbourn. Mr Gardiner is a sensible, gentlemanlike man, greatly superior to his sister, as much by nature as education. Mrs Gardiner is several years younger than Mrs Bennet and their other sister, Mrs Philips, and is an amiable, intelligent, elegant woman – a great favourite with all her Longbourn nieces.

During their stay, Wickham is often of your party and as Mrs Gardiner spent a considerable time, about ten years ago, in that very part of Derbyshire to which he belongs, they find they know many people in common and he is able to give her fresher intelligence of her former friends than she has been in the way of procuring. Since you value her opinion highly, it delights you to see your aunt enjoying Wickham's company. When you later acquaint her with Mr Darcy's treatment of Wickham, she tries to remember something of that gentleman's reputed disposition while a lad which might agree with your report, and is confident at last that she recollects having heard Mr Fitzwilliam Darcy formerly spoken of as a very proud, ill-natured boy.

*B*efore leaving Hertfordshire, Mrs Gardiner cautions you against Mr Wickham.

'You are too sensible a girl, Lizzy, to fall in love merely because you are warned against it; and, therefore, I am not afraid of speaking openly. Seriously, I would have you be on your guard. Do not involve yourself, or endeavour to involve him, in an affection which the want of fortune would make so very imprudent. I have nothing to say against *him*: he is a most interesting young man; and if he had the fortune he ought to have, I should think you could not do better. But as it is – you must not let your fancy run away with you. You have sense, and we all expect you to use it. Your father would depend on *your* resolution and good conduct, I am sure. You must not disappoint your father.'

You know that her advice is sound, though you do not readily wish to admit it: it irks you that want of fortune should be the sole means of preventing a match where there is a genuine meeting of minds. Though you tease her a little, however, you at last agree to do as she thinks wisest, or at least not *remind* your mother to invite him to the house so often. Your aunt is satisfied and now turns her thoughts and concern towards Jane.

'Do you think she would be prevailed on to go back with us?' she asks. 'A change of scene might be of service – and perhaps a little relief from home may be as useful as anything.'

Your mother's other sister, your aunt Philips, is apparently of the same view; at about this time Jane receives an invitation, extended to include you, to join her and your uncle on a trip to Bath.

Jane must now choose between London and Bath and asks your advice. You are not sure if it is wise for her to go to London, where she might see Mr Bingley and be reminded of her recent disappointment.

If you think she should go to London anyway, confident that Mr Darcy would never suffer his friend to visit Jane in such a part of London as Gracechurch Street, turn to page 82.

If you think a change of scene would do her good, but that she might suffer from being separated from her closest family for so long, turn to page 76 to accompany her to London yourself.

If you think it best to stay away from London and the Bingleys and that the waters at Bath might restore Jane's spirits, turn to page 92 to accept the Philipses' invitation.

You accept Mr Lefroy's proposal. Unfortunately, however, his great-uncle does not approve of the match on the grounds that Tom has five older sisters to support and is already indebted to his great-uncle for funding his studies in law. The expectations of the whole family are laid on him and under pressure from his family he is made to see that he cannot possibly risk his future by attaching himself to someone as woefully poor as you. He withdraws his offer, is whisked away swiftly from London by his great-uncle, and you are left to mend your broken heart.

Continue on page 91.

You agree that a change of scene would be of great service to Jane but fear she would suffer from being separated from you at this difficult time. You think it best to accompany her to your aunt Gardiner's in London. It is decided: on Saturday morning you are to set forth.

You arrive at the Gardiners' house in Gracechurch Street in excellent time and soon feel that the change of scene is as welcome to you as it must be to Jane. Your first day in London passes pleasantly away, the morning in bustle and shopping, and the evening at one of the theatres. You are delighted with London and your spirits are greatly revived. You congratulate yourself, in the light of your aunt's advice, on not thinking of Wickham at all.

The following evening you accompany your aunt and uncle to a large assembly in a fashionable part of town and you and Jane dress with care and attention, excited at the prospect of making new acquaintances. Shortly after your arrival, your host Mr King approaches and introduces you to a very gentlemanlike young Irishman from Dublin by the name of Mr Lefroy. He seems to be about two- or three-and-twenty, is tall, fair-haired, has a handsome and pleasing countenance, and a very intelligent and lively eye. You think he is perhaps the best-looking gentleman you have ever seen, even more handsome than Mr Wickham. He has already completed a degree in Dublin and is about to study for the Bar in London; his address is good, and you feel yourself in high luck. You begin to feel that accompanying Jane to London was a very fine scheme indeed.

There is little leisure for speaking while you dance, but when you are seated at tea, you find Mr Lefroy as agreeable as you already gave him credit for being. He talks with fluency and spirit – and there is an archness and pleasantry in his manner which immediately piques your interest. You wish to know more of Mr Lefroy. After talking for some time he suddenly, and with mock-seriousness, apologises for not having paid you the proper attentions expected of a partner.

'I have not yet asked you how long you have been in London; whether you were ever here before; whether you have been at the theatre, and the concert; and how you like the place altogether. I have been very negligent – but are you now at leisure to satisfy me in these particulars? If you are, I will begin directly.'

His tone and comic expression amuse you greatly and you are delighted to find that he considers the finer points of social etiquette as ridiculous as you do.

'You need not give yourself that trouble, sir,' you assure him with a smile, feeling that you understand one another well.

'No trouble, I assure you, madam,' says he, in reply. Then, forming his features into a set smile, and affectedly softening his voice, he adds, with a simpering air, 'Have you been long in London, madam?'

'Just two days, sir,' you reply, trying not to laugh at his perfect impression of a mannered gentleman of fashion.

Mr Lefroy affects astonishment. You take care to look

about you and see that nobody who might be offended by his impression might be standing by, but though you see many a specimen who could have been the model for this representation, none is standing near enough to hear. You turn back to Mr Lefroy with a smile. You wonder what he would have to say about the sombre Mr Darcy, and when you imagine Mr Lefroy doing an impression of *him* it is all you can do to stop yourself from laughing out loud. He continues to ask you in his affected tone whether you have been to the theatre and to the concert, and how well you like London so far.

'I like it very well,' is the only reply you can manage; you are trying extremely hard to contain your laughter.

'Now I must give one smirk,' says he, 'and then we may be rational again.'

You turn away to laugh. His satire on London society could not have been more in keeping with your own thinking, and his manner of expression diverts you exceedingly.

You are interrupted at this moment by Mrs Gardiner, with whom Mr Lefroy proceeds to converse with ease and elegance. Your admiration grows with every word he speaks, but you fear your aunt will not approve of this attachment: Mr Lefroy still has further studies to complete and has many financial obligations to his family. His prospects are therefore even worse than Wickham's.

You dance again; and you ask him what he thinks of books.

'I enjoy novels a great deal,' says he. 'But there has not been a tolerably decent one come out since *Tom Jones*.'

You can hardly believe it. A shared admiration of your favourite novel, added to his handsome countenance, gentlemanly manner, wit, playfulness and skill at dancing makes Thomas Langlois Lefroy the most charming man you have ever had the good fortune to meet, and when the assembly closes you part, on your side at least, with a strong inclination for continuing the acquaintance. Though you met but a few hours ago, you feel as if you have known him many months and go away with your head and heart full of Mr Lefroy.

That evening you share your feelings for Mr Lefroy with Jane. 'I mean to confine myself in future to Mr Tom Lefroy, for whom I do not care sixpence,' you say with good humour.

Jane is pleased that you are happy, and finds much to praise in him.

The following week you accompany your aunt to another ball, this time without Jane, who is prevented from attending by a violent toothache. You see Mr Lefroy again and feel that you have not been thinking of him with even the smallest degree of unreasonable admiration. He is everything you remembered him as being, and more. You are troubled to learn that he is to leave London the following Friday, but remind yourself that in affairs of the heart, much can happen in a few short days.

You return home that evening, flushed with happiness and wine, and Jane asks you how the evening passed.

'I am almost afraid to tell you how my Irish friend and I behaved,' you tease her. 'Imagine to yourself everything most profligate and shocking in the way of dancing and sitting down together. I *can* expose myself however, only *once more*,' you reassure her, 'because he leaves the country soon after next Friday.'

'Take care, Lizzy,' cautions Jane. 'However attached to you he may be himself, with studies to complete, and obligations to his family, he is not necessarily free to pay his attentions where he wishes.'

You know she is right, though you do not wish to admit it. Her advice reminds you of that given to you by your aunt Gardiner as she cautioned you against Mr Wickham, and though you are familiar with the ways of the world and what they must mean for you, this does not prevent you from being vexed by them.

Though you promise to, you cannot hide your admiration for Mr Lefroy; his manifold attractions are more persuasive than Jane's reasoning. He can hide his affections no better than you, and before his departure from London he pays you a visit and makes you an offer of marriage.

If you wish to accept his attractive offer, turn to page 75.

If you wish to refuse him, turn to page 144 and steel your heart against him.

*Y*ou approve of your aunt Gardiner's scheme and tell her you are confident Jane will accept the invitation.

'I hope,' adds Mrs Gardiner, 'that no consideration with regard to Mr Bingley will influence her. We live in so different a part of town, all our connections are so different, and, as you well know, we go out so little, that it is very improbable they should meet at all, unless he really comes to see her.'

'And *that* is quite impossible,' you reply, 'for he is now in the custody of his friend, and Mr Darcy would no more suffer him to call on Jane in such a part of London! My dear aunt, how could you think of it? Mr Darcy may, perhaps, have *heard* of such a place as Gracechurch Street, but he would hardly think a month's ablution enough to cleanse him from its impurities, were he once to enter it; and, depend upon it, Mr Bingley never stirs without him.'

'So much the better,' replies your aunt. 'I hope they will not meet at all. But does not Jane correspond with his sister? *She* will not be able to help calling.'

'She will drop the acquaintance entirely,' you reply.

Although you are certain in your belief that Mr Darcy would never allow Bingley to call on Jane, you still do not consider the situation entirely hopeless. It is possible, and sometimes you think it probable, that Bingley's affection might be reanimated, and the influence of his friends successfully combated by the more natural influence of Jane's attractions, should they meet again.

Jane accepts your aunt's invitation with pleasure, and they set off for London in high spirits the following Saturday. As she leaves, you urge Jane to write as soon as possible, secretly hoping that she will soon be able to send favourable news of Bingley. You will miss your sister, and once you have watched the carriage leave, you turn back to the house with a heavy heart. With Jane gone and Charlotte soon to follow, you will soon be at a loss for intelligent company. You therefore resolve to apply yourself to your work with more than usual vigour so as to leave no time for sad reflections.

Proceed to page 104.

A few days later, you and Jane receive an invitation from the Westons to join them for a day trip and picnic at a picturesque location a few miles from Meryton. You accept the invitation and look forward to it with pleasure. Maria has likewise been invited and seems particularly keen to make an impression, going so far as to ask your advice on what she should wear, which you put down to her growing attachment to Mr Frank Churchill, who will also be in attendance.

When Saturday comes the weather is very hot indeed, and you are in high spirits. You set off for your picnic in anticipation of a very pleasant day and you, Mr Knightley, the Bateses, Jane Fairfax, your sister Jane, Frank, the Westons and the Lucases reach your destination in time for a short walk before picnicking.

Frank Churchill is talkative and gay over lunch, making you his first object. After chatting for some time amongst companions almost silent due to the oppressive heat, Frank leans towards you and whispers, 'Our companions are excessively stupid. What shall we do to rouse them?' He evidently thinks of something at once as he suddenly turns towards the general company and embarrasses you by making a loud announcement.

'Ladies and gentlemen,' says he, 'I am ordered by Miss Bennet to say that she demands, by way of entertainment, from each of you either one thing very clever, be it prose or verse, original or repeated, or two things moderately clever, or three things very dull indeed, and she engages to laugh heartily at them all.'

Though you find him amusing, you wish he had not said it all in your name. From your sister Jane's alarmed and concerned expression you see that she, at least, knows you would never have said such a thing yourself. You do your best to hide a blush.

'Oh! Very well,' exclaims Miss Bates, 'then I need not be uneasy. "Three things very dull indeed." That will just do for me, you know. I shall be sure to say three dull things as soon as ever I open my mouth, shan't I?' she says, looking round with the most good-humoured dependence on everybody's assent. 'Do not you all think I shall?'

You are amused by her light-hearted satirical self-awareness, and, inspired by Frank's audaciousness, cannot resist a retort.

'Ah! Ma'am, but there may be a difficulty,' you say with a smile. 'Pardon me, but you will be limited as to number – only three at once.'

Everyone is silent, and you instantly regret what you have said.

Miss Bates, deceived by the mock ceremony of your manner, does not immediately catch your meaning; but, when it bursts on her, a slight blush shows that it pains her.

'Ah! Well – to be sure. Yes, I see what she means,' she says, turning to Mr Knightley, 'and I will try to hold my tongue. I must make myself very disagreeable, or she would not have said such a thing to an old friend.'

Mr Knightley is very grave; Lady Lucas excuses herself by saying she has no pleasure from such diversions; and Jane Fairfax offers her aunt her arm.

'Now, ma'am,' says she to Miss Bates, 'shall we join Lady Lucas?'

They walk off, followed in half a minute by Mr Knightley, who takes your sister Jane with him, though she is reluctant to leave you at such a time. You wish that you had not been so influenced by Mr Churchill's insouciance, but earnestly hope that your joke will soon be forgotten.

You are left to the flattery of Mr Churchill and the conversation of Maria, which all at once you find insipid and extremely dull, and the appearance of the servants looking out for you to give notice of the carriages is, therefore, a joyful sight.

While waiting for the carriage, you suddenly find Mr Knightley by your side. He seems to have something particular to say to you, and looks around as if to see that no one is near before speaking. You fear he has come to criticise you, and your fears are not unjust. He prefaces his speech by saying that he cannot see you acting wrong without a remonstrance, and that he claims the privilege of speaking to you as he used to do.

'How could you be so unfeeling to Miss Bates?' he continues. 'How could you be so insolent in your wit to a woman of her character, age and situation?'

You blush, are sorry, but try to laugh it off.

'Nay, how could I help saying what I did?' you reply.

'Nobody could have helped it. It was not so very bad. I dare say she did not understand me.'

You rather hope than believe it to be true.

'I assure you she did,' says Mr Knightley. 'She felt your full meaning. She has talked of it since. I wish you could have heard how she talked of it – with what candour and generosity – honouring your forbearance in being able to pay her such attentions as she was forever receiving from yourself, when her society must be so irksome.'

You feel all the force of his criticism, but still you feel you must defend yourself. You were wrong to say it, but you did not say anything but what everybody present was thinking. You endeavour to shake off the gravity of the situation by saying that though there is not a better creature in the world, even Mr Knightley must allow that what is good and what is ridiculous are most unfortunately blended in her. But Mr Knightley is not so easily appeased.

'They are blended,' says he, 'I acknowledge; and, were she prosperous, I could allow much for the occasional prevalence of the ridiculous over the good. But consider her situation, and how unequal it is to your own. She is poor; she has sunk from the comforts she was born to; and, if she lives to an old age, must probably sink more. Her situation should secure your compassion. It was badly done, indeed! To have you laugh at her, humble her – and before her niece, too.'

To have upset Miss Bates is bad enough, and you now regret it deeply, but Mr Knightley's disapprobation humiliates you beyond expression. The carriage draws up and before you can speak again, he has handed you in. Never have you felt so agitated, mortified, grieved, at any circumstance in your life.

The wretchedness of the scene at the picnic is in your thoughts the whole evening long and on Jane's advice, the following morning you pay a visit to the Bateses to make amends for your insulting blunder. Miss Fairfax does not leave her room, and though Miss Bates is polite, there is not the same cheerful volubility as before, and you feel the change deeply.

You enquire after Miss Fairfax, and are told that she has just accepted a position as governess to a family living at some distance from Meryton. To be forced by reduced circumstances to take a position as governess must be a hard lot indeed for one raised as highly as Miss Fairfax has been, and for the first time you feel genuine compassion for her. You offer good wishes to Miss Bates, who thanks you for your kindness.

You return home to find that Mr Knightley has arrived during your absence. You are sure Mr Knightley has not forgiven you; his behaviour is not what it usually is. Time, you console yourself, will tell him that you ought to be friends again. While he stands as if meaning to go, your mother begins her enquiries.

'And how did you find my old friend and her daughter? Lizzy has been to call on the Bateses and Miss Fairfax, Mr Knightley. She is always so attentive to them,' she says, all smiling attention to Mr Knightley.

Your colour is heightened by this unjust praise; and with a smile, and shake of the head, which speaks much, you look at Mr Knightley. All that has passed of good in your feelings, however, is at once caught and honoured. He looks at you with a glow of regard. You are warmly gratified – and in another moment still more so, by a little movement of more than common friendliness on his part. He takes your hand, presses it, and certainly is on the point of carrying it to his lips when, from some fancy or other, he suddenly lets it go. Why he should feel such a scruple, why he should change his mind when it was all but done, you cannot perceive. The intention, however, is indubitable; and you cannot but recall the attempt with great satisfaction. He tells you that he will be away visiting his brother in London for some days, and embarks immediately afterwards.

Mr Churchill has been in London since the picnic, and the day following Mr Knightley's departure thither, Mrs Weston receives a letter from Frank giving the news of the death of his aunt. Frank is now free to do as he pleases and marry where he likes – a blessing for Maria – and you are delighted for him. Maria seems very happy to hear this latest news, which only confirms your suspicions about her feelings for him. Although you have never seen him show any particular attention to her, you hope for her sake that he will begin to notice her now, and see beyond her plain looks to appreciate the sweet-natured girl within. You vow once again to praise her many good qualities next time you speak with Mr Churchill. She deserves a good husband, and with youth on her side, you feel that with a little help she has a chance to make a better match than her sister Charlotte.

Continue on page 124.

*Y*ou judge it best to remove yourself from London and all its reminders of your recent, but sadly deceased, happiness. Jane is prevailed upon to stay by your aunt and uncle, and as you take leave of her, you think that though you have not yet met with them, she must surely soon be reunited with the Bingleys. Reflecting on this gives you great comfort and you journey home to Longbourn in good spirits.

When you are safely back in Hertfordshire your thoughts turn to Charlotte and her forthcoming marriage to your cousin Mr Collins. You will miss her friendship and society dearly, and feel a great deal of pity and compassion for her when you imagine what her life as Mrs Collins will be like. It was her choice, however; she has chosen her fate and there is nothing to do now but wait for the wedding to seal it.

Proceed to page 104.

*Y*ou decide that it would be best for Jane not to go to London, but agree that a change of scene would do her good. You both accept the invitation from your aunt and uncle Philips and all set off for Bath the following Saturday.

You make your appearance in the Lower Rooms on the third evening of your visit; and here fortune is favourable to you. The master of ceremonies introduces to you a very gentlemanlike young man by the name of Henry Tilney. He seems to be about four- or five-and-twenty, is rather tall, has a pleasing countenance, a very intelligent and lively eye, and, if not quite handsome, is very near it. He is a clergyman of a very respectable family in Gloucestershire whose mother, you learn, died some years ago. Though he is not as handsome as Mr Wickham, there is something in his manner that speaks of a quickness that Wickham was sometimes without and you feel all the good fortune of meeting him now, when you are most in need of distraction and diversion.

Mr Tilney introduces you and Jane to his father and sister and you are pleased with them both. Eleanor is every bit as charming as her brother and has a good figure and pretty face. Their father, General Tilney, is a very handsome man, of a commanding aspect, past the bloom, but not past the vigour of life. You introduce them to the Philipses and everyone is delighted with each other.

'What a handsome family they are!' Jane whispers to you as the Tilneys are talking to your aunt and uncle.

You couldn't agree more.

You dance and converse with Mr Tilney for most of the evening, and are impressed and charmed by his wit and intelligence. While you are seated at tea he launches into such a humorous and satirical impression of the usual social discourse at such events that you cannot refrain from laughing.

'I see what you think of me,' he says gravely, 'I shall make but a poor figure in your journal tomorrow.'

'My journal!' you cry.

'Yes, I know exactly what you will say: Friday, went to the Lower Rooms; wore my sprigged muslin robe with blue trimmings – plain black shoes – appeared to much advantage; but was strangely harassed by a queer, half-witted man, who would make me dance with him, and distressed me by his nonsense.'

'Indeed I shall say no such thing.'

'Shall I tell you what you ought to say?'

'If you please.'

'I danced with a very agreeable young man, introduced by Mr King; had a great deal of conversation with him – seems a most extraordinary genius – hope I may know more of him. *That*, madam, is what I *wish* you to say.'

You turn your head so as not to show it, but you cannot help but be charmed. You discover that he loves the Gothic novels of Mrs Radcliffe, and he recommends one or two of them for you to read. It is a genre of literature you thought laughable in the past, but a recommendation from Mr Tilney is enough to make you reconsider it. You go home that night thinking of Mr Tilney, and have high hopes of meeting him again at tomorrow evening's cotillion ball.

Your hopes are not disappointed. When you enter the ballroom the following evening you soon find yourself addressed and solicited to dance by Mr Tilney and you grant his request with pleasure.

From this time forward, you spend as many of your days as possible with the Tilneys, and your regard for the brother gradually increases. You obtain copies of Mrs Radcliffe's novels *The Romance of the Forest* and *The Mysteries of Udolpho* as recommended, and find that you cannot put them down. Against all your better judgement you are forced to confess yourself an admirer of Gothic literature.

*O*ne morning, just as you are reflecting on how pleasant it is for you to now have friends in Bath, Miss Tilney informs you of her father's plans to leave town by the end of the week. You are very sorry for it, but you do not have long to lament your bad luck, for Miss Tilney proceeds to invite you to accompany them to their family home, Northanger Abbey. Having recently read a great deal of Gothic literature, you find the prospect of staying in a real-life abbey quite exciting. You are reluctant to leave Jane, but she assures you that she is well and happy, and greatly enjoying the society that Bath affords. Your aunt and uncle agree to part with you, and you therefore accept Eleanor's invitation and set off in Henry's curricle at the appointed time the following Saturday.

You arrive at the abbey in good time and Miss Tilney shows you to your apartment. It is all disappointingly modern and not at all what you have been led to expect from the Gothic novels you have read. Despite yourself, you cannot help feeling a little disenchanted. You dress quickly for dinner and hurry down to the drawing room, where the General is pacing, his watch in his hand and, on the very instant of your entering, pulls the bell with violence and orders: 'Dinner to be on the table directly!' His temper seems unreasonably short and you begin to wonder whether your stay at Northanger is going to be quite as pleasant as you had anticipated. You had not thought it possible, but General Tilney seems to be even more bad-tempered than Mr Darcy.

*T*he following morning Mr Tilney leaves for London, where business will keep him for some days. You are a little disappointed to see him go, but your mood is brightened when Eleanor and the General propose a tour of the abbey. You begin with the gardens, and before long you come to a narrow path that winds through a thick grove of old Scotch firs. It is dark and shady, and you are struck by its gloomy aspect. To your surprise, the General excuses himself from attending you, saying that he prefers to be in the sun, and will meet you by another course.

'I am particularly fond of this spot,' says Miss Tilney as you turn in to the grove. 'It was my mother's favourite walk.'

Mrs Tilney is so rarely mentioned in the family that your interest is piqued by this tender remembrance. It seems to you a little odd that the General should have excused himself from entering the grove if it was Mrs Tilney's favourite walk, but you think little of it. Miss Tilney goes on to tell you that she was only thirteen when her mother died, and you are struck by the sadness of the story. You are curious to know more about Mrs Tilney, and with every answer your questions receive, your interest in her augments. From what Eleanor says, and from your own observations of the General's temper, you begin to feel persuaded that Mrs Tilney was unhappy in marriage. Your instincts tell you it must have been so.

The end of the path brings you directly upon the General, and you find yourself again obliged to walk with him. Though you smile and talk with him as before, you cannot put your thoughts concerning Mrs Tilney's unhappiness entirely from your mind. You wish to know more about her and the circumstances of her death, and resolve to ask Eleanor for further details when next you are alone.

You finish your tour of the gardens and return to the abbey, where your tour resumes. You ascend the chief staircase and turn in an opposite direction from the gallery in which your room lies. Miss Tilney is just about to open a door to the left when her father the General comes forward and calls her hastily and rather angrily back, demanding to know where she is going, and affirming that you have surely already seen all that can be worth your notice. He clearly wishes to conceal something, and what that something is, a short sentence of Miss Tilney's seems to point out: 'I was going to take you into what was my mother's room – the room in which she died.' You wonder what Mrs Radcliffe would have to say about the General's behaviour. He seems reluctant to venture anywhere that might remind him of his late wife, and you begin to wonder if it does not spring from his own sense of guilt concerning his behaviour towards her during her illness. Your suspicions are aroused and you grow more and more convinced that the General was a hard, unfeeling husband.

You venture, when next alone with Miss Tilney, to express your wish of being permitted to see her mother's room, as well as all the rest of that side of the house; and she promises to attend you there, whenever there is a convenient hour. You guess at her meaning: that the General must be away from home before that room can be entered. Such hints only compound your growing suspicions. You ask her if the room remains as it was, and when she replies in the affirmative, you cannot refrain from going on to ask if she was with her mother to the last.

'No,' replies Miss Tilney, 'I was unfortunately from home. Her illness was sudden and short, and it was all over before I arrived.'

Your blood runs cold with the suggestions which naturally spring from these words. Could Henry's father . . .? Could it be possible? It hardly bears thinking about, but you find that you cannot put the awful possibility from your mind. You resolve at last to discover the truth, and think that your best chance of success lies in gaining admittance to Mrs Tilney's room, which might yet hold some clue as to what happened in those final days leading up to her death. To your disappointment, though you hope to be shown her apartment soon, no opportunity arises.

*A*t last, you decide to attempt the forbidden door alone and at four o'clock you retire to dress half an hour earlier than usual. You find yourself alone in the gallery before the clocks cease to strike. You slip with the least possible noise through the folding doors of the gallery, and without stopping, hurry forward to the door in question. The lock yields to your hand. On tiptoe you enter, and the room is before you. You see a large, well-proportioned apartment, a handsome bed, mahogany wardrobes and neatly painted chairs, on which the warm beams of a western sun gaily pour through two sash windows. You are shocked at first, and then deeply mortified. You hardly know what scene of horror you expected to behold, or what possible proof of the General's cruelty could ever have been found there; but it is clear that you have been grossly mistaken in everything.

Common sense returns to you and you feel bitterly ashamed of yourself. You feel that none of this ever would have happened if you hadn't been influenced by Mrs Radcliffe's novels, and you regret the day you ever set eyes on them. You are sick of exploring, and want only to be safe in the solitude of your own room. You are on the point of retreating, when the sound of footsteps stops you in your tracks. To be found there, even by a servant, would be unpleasant; but by the General, much worse. You listen, but the sound has ceased. Resolving not to lose a moment, you pass through the door and close it behind you.

At that instant a door underneath is hastily opened and someone begins to ascend the stairs with swift steps. You have no power to move. With a feeling of panic, you fix your eyes on the staircase.

Turn to page 115.

*M*ore than once in your ramble within the park do you unexpectedly meet Mr Darcy. To prevent its ever happening again, you take care to inform him at first that it is a favourite haunt of yours. How it could occur a second time, therefore, is very odd! Yet it does, and even a third.

You are engaged one day, as you walk, in re-perusing Jane's last letter when you are surprised not by Mr Darcy, but Colonel Fitzwilliam. You are always pleased to see him, and you walk together towards the parsonage. He tells you that he and his cousin are to leave Kent on Saturday to visit Miss Darcy of whom, you learn, they are joint guardians. You are happy to tell him that you have heard a great deal of praise of her from Miss Bingley. Although Colonel Fitzwilliam is not well acquainted with that lady, he knows of her brother through Mr Darcy.

'From something that he told me in our journey hither,' says the Colonel, 'I have reason to think Bingley very much indebted to him.' He stops himself. 'But I ought to beg his pardon, for I have no right to suppose that Bingley was the person meant. It was all conjecture.'

'What is it you mean?' you ask, your curiosity piqued.

'It is a circumstance which Darcy of course could not wish to be generally known,' says the Colonel, 'because if it were to get round to the lady's family it would be an unpleasant thing.'

'You may depend upon my not mentioning it,' you reply.

'What he told me was merely this: that he congratulated himself on having lately saved a friend from the inconveniences of a most imprudent marriage, but without mentioning names or any other particulars; and I only suspected it to be Bingley from believing him the kind of young man to get into a scrape of that sort, and from knowing them to have been together the whole of last summer.'

The colour rises in your cheeks. Though you have long suspected it, you can hardly believe what you have heard. Shock, anger and disbelief overwhelm you.

'Did Mr Darcy give you his reasons for this interference?' you say, struggling to conceal your agitation.

'I understood that there were some very strong objections against the lady,' he replies.

Your heart swells with indignation.

'I do not see what right Mr Darcy had to decide on the propriety of his friend's inclination,' you exclaim with passion, but recollecting yourself, you abruptly change the conversation and talk on indifferent matters till you reach the parsonage.

You shut yourself in the drawing room where you can think without interruption of all that you have heard, and the agitation and tears which the subject occasion bring on a violent headache. You are thinking of Mr Darcy with anger and resentment when you are suddenly roused by the sound of the doorbell. To your utter amazement, you see Mr Darcy walk into the room. You can hardly believe your misfortune. He is the last person you could wish to see at this moment and you greet him with cold civility. He sits down for a few moments, and then getting up, walks about the room. Though you are surprised by his pacing about the room, you say not a word. You can think of no one with whom you could wish to converse less, and have not the slightest inclination to ease his discomfort by finding a subject upon which to talk. After an awkward silence of several minutes, he comes towards you in an agitated manner, and thus begins: 'In vain have I struggled. It will not do. My feelings will not be repressed. You must allow me to tell you how ardently I admire and love you.'

Your astonishment is beyond expression. You stare, colour, doubt, and are silent. This he considers sufficient encouragement, and the avowal of all that he feels, and has long felt, for you immediately follows. He speaks well; but there are feelings besides those of the heart to be detailed: his sense of your inferiority – of its being a degradation – of the family obstacles which have, until this moment, prevented him from making his feelings known to you, are dwelt on with warmth.

Your resentment rises. You try, however, to compose yourself so as to answer him with patience when he has done cataloguing your faults. He concludes by representing to you the strength of that attachment which, in spite of all his endeavours, he has found impossible to conquer, and by expressing his hope that it will now be rewarded by your acceptance of his hand.

To accept Mr Darcy's proposal, turn to page 132. He might not be particularly eloquent, but this is an offer you cannot refuse given your family circumstances.

To refuse his offer, turn to page 119. You'd rather die in penury than marry Mr Darcy.

*T*he day of Charlotte and Mr Collins's wedding approaches and on her final night of liberty Miss Lucas comes to say goodbye. She invites you to Hunsford and though you foresee little pleasure in the visit, you consent to be of the party when Sir William and Charlotte's sister, Maria, visit her in March. The wedding takes place and the bride and bridegroom set off for Kent from the church door. You are sorry to see your friend go.

The following day, you receive a letter from Jane in London. You had hoped to hear something of the Bingleys, but your hopes are disappointed. A further four weeks pass before you receive news from Jane that Miss Bingley has finally visited her and that her manner towards your sister was greatly altered when she did. She implied to Jane that Mr Bingley knows she is in town, but is kept away by his partiality for Miss Darcy; and furthermore, that Bingley is never to return to Netherfield and will most likely give up the house. In the light of this, all hope for Mr Bingley and Jane is now absolutely over; and Mr Bingley's character sinks in your estimation on every review of it.

About this time Mrs Gardiner reminds you in a letter of your promise not to encourage Mr Wickham's attentions. She requires information about him and you have such to send as might rather give contentment to your aunt than to yourself. You have heard from your aunt Philips that Wickham has been paying his attentions to someone else. The sudden acquisition of ten thousand pounds is the most remarkable charm of the young lady, Miss King, to whom he is now rendering himself agreeable. His apparent partiality for you has subsided.

Though you cannot help feeling something very near jealousy when you hear the news, your sisters Kitty and Lydia take Wickham's defection much more to heart than you do. They are young in the ways of the world, and not yet open to the mortifying conviction that handsome young men must have something to live on as well as the plain.

March arrives and you set off to visit Charlotte in Kent with Sir William and Maria. You spend the night at the Gardiners' house in London on your way and are pleased to see that Jane does not suffer from her disappointments: she is as healthful and lovely as ever. The day passes away most pleasantly and that evening you have the unexpected happiness of an invitation to accompany your uncle and aunt Gardiner in a tour of pleasure which they propose taking in the summer.

'We have not quite determined how far it shall carry us,' says your aunt, 'but, perhaps, to the Lakes.'

Your acceptance of the invitation is most ready and grateful. You feel all the advantage of having something to look forward to, and feel certain that the picturesque beauty of the area will distract you from all thoughts of Wickham.

'My dear, dear aunt,' you rapturously cry, 'what delight!

What felicity! You give me fresh life and vigour. Adieu to disappointment and spleen. What are men to rocks and mountains?'

⌒

Good question. A trip to the Lakes is likely to prove a great test of your appreciation of the picturesque. Take the following Picturesque Appreciation Test to see if you are truly ready for a trip to the Lake District.

Which of the following best describes you?

a) You are not really fond of nettles, thistles or heath blossoms. You prefer tall and flourishing trees to those which are crooked and blasted; neat to ruined cottages; and snug farmhouses to Gothic watchtowers.

b) You are fond of nettles and thistles but not heath blossoms; and though you quite like Gothic watchtowers in principle, you wouldn't want to live in one.

c) You have read William Gilpin's essays on the picturesque forty times over and admire a good view so much that if it were interrupted by something that did not perfectly accord with your idea of the picturesque, you would immediately set about destroying it; even if that something were the entire city of Bath.

If you answered a), turn to page 114.

If you answered b), turn to page 145.

If you answered c), turn to page 135.

The following day you leave London for Kent, satisfied that Jane is happy and healthy. At length you reach the village of Hunsford and the parsonage is discernible, and Mr Collins and Charlotte appear at the door. With no other delay than Mr Collins's pointing out the neatness of the entrance, you are taken into the house.

You were prepared to see him in his full glory, and you cannot help fancying that in displaying the good proportions of the room, its aspect and its furniture, he addresses himself particularly to you, as if wishing to make you feel what you have lost in refusing him.

'We dine at Rosings twice every week,' boasts Mr Collins, 'and are never allowed to walk home. Lady Catherine's carriage is regularly ordered for us. I *should* say, *one* of her Ladyship's carriages, for she has several.' The following day Mr Collins's triumph is complete when Lady Catherine, as anticipated, sends an invitation to dinner, and scarcely anything else is talked of the whole day. While you and Maria are dressing that evening, Mr Collins comes two or three times to your different doors to recommend your being quick as Lady Catherine very much objects to being kept waiting for her dinner. Such formidable accounts of her Ladyship and her manner of living quite frighten Maria, who has been little used to company, and when you approach the house after the half-mile walk across the park, her alarm increases at every moment. Even Sir William does not look quite calm, but you find your courage does not fail you. You have heard nothing of Lady Catherine that speaks her awful from any extraordinary talents or miraculous virtue, and the mere stateliness of money and rank you think you can witness without trepidation.

The servants show you in, and Charlotte makes the introduction. Sir William, despite having been presented at St James's, is so completely awed by the grandeur surrounding him that he has only courage enough to make a very low bow and take his seat without saying a word. Maria, frightened almost out of her senses, sits on the edge of her chair, not knowing which way to look. You, however, find yourself quite equal to the scene, and observe the two ladies before you composedly.

Lady Catherine you find to be a tall, large woman, with strongly marked features, which might once have been handsome. Miss de Bourgh, by contrast, is pale and sickly; her features, though not plain, are insignificant; and she speaks very little. Though not rendered formidable by silence, whatever Lady Catherine says is spoken in so authoritative a tone as to mark her self-importance, and by the end of half an hour's acquaintance you have determined that in countenance and deportment she exactly resembles her nephew, Mr Darcy.

Though the company leaves much to be desired, the dinner is exceedingly handsome, and after dinner you return to the drawing room with the ladies of the group, where there is little to be done but to submit to Lady Catherine's interrogations, during which she discovers, to her horror, that not only were you and your sisters raised without a governess, but all five of you are 'out' at once.

'All!' she cries. 'What, all five out at once? Very odd! And you only the second. The younger ones out before the elder are married! Your younger sisters must be very young?'

'Yes,' you reply, 'my youngest is not sixteen. Perhaps *she* is full young to be much in company. But really, ma'am, I think it would be very hard upon younger sisters that they should not have their share of society and amusement, because the elder may not have the means or inclination to marry early. The last born has as good a right to the pleasures of youth as the first. And to be kept back on *such* a motive! I think it would not be very likely to promote sisterly affection or delicacy of mind.'

'Upon my word,' says her Ladyship, 'you give your opinion very decidedly for so young a person. Pray, what is your age?'

'With three younger sisters grown up,' you reply, smiling, 'your Ladyship can hardly expect me to own it.'

Lady Catherine seems quite astonished at not receiving a direct answer, and you suspect yourself to be the first creature who has ever dared to trifle with so much dignified impertinence.

You are saved the indignity of further questioning by the arrival of the gentlemen, and after tea the card tables are placed. The rest of the evening is spent rather stupidly, with scarcely a syllable being uttered that does not relate to the game, until Lady Catherine and her daughter have played as much as they like, at which point the carriage is at last offered, and you and your party return to the parsonage.

$\mathcal{S}$ir William stays only a week in Kent; but his visit is long enough to convince him of his elder daughter's being most comfortably settled, and of her possessing such a husband and such a neighbour as are not often met with. Despite the evenings spent at Rosings, upon the whole you spend your time comfortably enough at Hunsford, in conversation with Charlotte, or walking with Maria. In this quiet way the first fortnight of your visit soon passes away. You then learn that Mr Darcy is expected at Rosings for Easter and can hardly believe your bad luck.

Darcy brings with him his cousin, a Colonel Fitzwilliam, and to your great surprise they both pay a visit to you at the parsonage shortly after arriving. Colonel Fitzwilliam is about thirty, not quite as handsome as Darcy, but in person and address most truly the gentleman. You are struck by the great difference between the two gentlemen; while Colonel Fitzwilliam enters into conversation with readiness and ease, his cousin sits without speaking to anybody. At length, however, Mr Darcy asks after the health of your family. You give the customary answer, and after a moment's pause, decide to ask him whether he has seen Jane in town. You know he has not, but wish to see how he reacts to the question: you are still convinced that Darcy and Miss Bingley have concealed from Mr Bingley their knowledge of Jane's being in London. Darcy looks a little confused as he answers that he has not been so fortunate as to see Miss Bennet. You pursue the subject no further, and the gentlemen soon afterwards go away.

The following morning, you are sitting by yourself and writing to Jane, when you are startled by a knock at the front door. The housemaid opens it and in a few moments, to your very great surprise, Mr Darcy, and Mr Darcy only, enters the room. He too seems astonished on finding you alone: he had understood all the ladies to be within. You both sit down, and seem in danger of sinking into total silence. It is absolutely necessary, therefore, to think of something to say. The first thing that comes to mind are your suspicions concerning his part in Bingley's departure from Netherfield, and as your feelings of resentment against him rise up in you, you cannot help exclaiming abruptly, 'How very suddenly you all quitted Netherfield last November, Mr Darcy! I think I have understood that Mr Bingley has not much idea of ever returning to Netherfield again?'

'Yes,' replies Darcy, 'I should not be surprised if he were to give it up as soon as any eligible property becomes available.'

You make no answer. You are afraid of talking longer of his friend lest you should overcome the boundaries of decorum and accuse him outright of ruining your sister's happiness.

Mr Darcy draws back his chair, takes a newspaper from the table, and, glancing over it, says, in a colder voice, 'Are you pleased with Kent?'

A short dialogue on the subject of the country ensues, and he soon afterwards quits the house. Your mind is disturbed by his confusing and contrary behaviour. 'What can he mean by it?' you ask yourself, until you grow so frustrated that you vow to waste no more time thinking unnecessarily about a man for whom you care very little indeed.

After this bewildering visit from Mr Darcy, he and his cousin find a reason to walk to the parsonage almost every day. It is clear that Colonel Fitzwilliam visits you because he has pleasure in your society, but why Mr Darcy comes so often to the parsonage it is more difficult to understand. Charlotte thinks he must be in love with you and watches him carefully. While he certainly looks at you a great deal, however, the expression of that look is disputable: sometimes it seems nothing but absence of mind.

Continue on page 100.

*Y*ou have no appreciation of the picturesque at all and are woefully underprepared for a trip to the Lakes. Procure a copy of William Gilpin's essays immediately and do not proceed north until you have read them at least five times over.

Continue on page 108.

*I*n a few moments you are faced with Mr Tilney. You are extremely astonished to see him, and know not how to even begin explaining yourself to him.

'How came you here? How came you up that staircase?' you ask hastily in some confusion.

He looks astonished too, and explains in a tone of great surprise that it is the nearest way from the stable yard to his own chamber. You recollect yourself, blush, and can say no more. You move on towards the gallery, eager to be gone, but Mr Tilney stops you by asking in turn, how *you* came to be there. Avoiding his eye, you explain that you have been to see his mother's room and then do your best to change the subject. Mr Tilney is not taken in by your attempt, however, and asks you what you thought of his mother's room. He asks you if Eleanor sent you to see it, and 'No' is your only reply.

After a short silence, during which Mr Tilney closely observes you, he asks whether your curiosity to see the room proceeded from Eleanor's description of their mother's character, and whether Eleanor has talked of her a great deal.

'Yes. No. That is, not so much,' you reply, floundering. 'But what she did say was very interesting. Her dying so suddenly,' you continue with some hesitation, 'and none of you being at home . . .'

Henry is quick to catch your meaning, and asks whether, from these circumstances, you have inferred the probability of some negligence, or, perhaps, something much worse. You are mortified beyond expression and can make no answer.

Mr Tilney explains that though the seizure which ended in his mother's death *was* sudden, the malady itself was one from which she had often suffered. During the progress of her disorder he saw her repeatedly, though Eleanor *was* absent, and at such a distance that sadly, when she retuned home, Mrs Tilney had died.

'But your father,' you ask, 'was *he* afflicted?'

'For a time, greatly so,' Mr Tilney replies. 'His value of her was sincere; and, if not permanently, he was truly afflicted by her death.'

'I am very glad of it,' you reply.

'If I understand you rightly,' replies Mr Tilney in some dismay, 'you had formed a surmise of such horror as I have hardly words to . . . Dear Miss Bennet, consider the dreadful nature of the suspicions you have entertained. What have you been judging from? Remember the country and the age in which we live. Remember that we are English, that we are Christians. Dearest Miss Bennet, what ideas have you been admitting?'

You return to your room in shame and embarrassment. It is not only with yourself that you are sunk – but with Henry too. Your folly has been exposed to him, and he must despise you forever. You earnestly regret ever having read Mrs Radcliffe's novels, and cannot help but laugh at the bitter irony that it was Mr Tilney who introduced you to them in the first place. You vow never to pick one up again for as long as you live. You hope that in time, Henry will learn to forgive you, and your indiscretion will be forgotten.

The following morning Eleanor comes to you in great distress to inform you that the General has recollected an engagement that takes the whole family away on Monday. Tomorrow morning is fixed for your leaving, and no servant will be offered you. It is clear that you have offended the General in some way, and it seems to you only too likely that he has somehow learnt of your suspicions regarding his part in his wife's death. You are deeply dismayed, and return home to Longbourn certain that you will never see Henry again.

You long to see Jane, but when you left Bath to visit the Tilneys, she travelled on to stay with the Gardiners in London. You are sure she will send you news by letter soon, however, and every morning is spent watching out for the post.

The company and conversation of your father helps you to forget your recent disappointment and before long you learn not to think of Mr Tilney.

Your thoughts soon turn towards Charlotte and her forthcoming marriage to your cousin Mr Collins. You will miss her friendship and society dearly, and feel a great deal of pity and compassion for her when you imagine what her life as Mrs Collins will be like. It was her choice, however. She has chosen her fate and there is nothing to do now but wait for the wedding to seal it.

Proceed to page 104.

You see that Mr Darcy has no doubt of a favourable answer. He *speaks* of apprehension and anxiety, but in his countenance you read smug security which only exasperates you further. That he should have taken the trouble to outline all his most insulting objections to you, combined with your knowledge of his part in separating Jane and Bingley, makes you angrier than you have perhaps ever before been in your life. When he ceases, you feel the colour rising in your cheeks, and you answer him by saying, 'In such cases as this, it is, I believe, the established mode to express a sense of obligation for the sentiments avowed, and if I could *feel* gratitude, I would now thank you. But I cannot – I have never desired your good opinion, and you have certainly bestowed it most unwillingly. I am sorry to have occasioned pain to anyone. It has been most unconsciously done, however, and I hope will be of short duration.'

Mr Darcy's surprise is evident. His complexion becomes pale with anger, and the disturbance of his mind is visible in every feature.

'And this,' says he, struggling for composure, 'is all the reply which I am to have the honour of expecting! I might, perhaps, wish to be informed why, with so little *endeavour* at civility, I am thus rejected. But it is of small importance.'

'I might as well enquire,' you reply, incensed at his unfaltering pride, 'why with so evident a design of offending and insulting me, you chose to tell me that you liked me against your will, against your reason and even against your character? And even if my own feelings had not decided against you, do you think that any consideration would tempt me to accept the man who has been the means of ruining, perhaps forever, the happiness of a most beloved sister?'

As you pronounce these words Mr Darcy changes colour. The emotion is short, however. He listens without attempting to interrupt you while you challenge him to deny that he has been the principal, if not the only, means of dividing Jane and Bingley from each other and involving them both in misery of the acutest kind. You pause, and see that he is listening with an air which proves him wholly unmoved by any feeling of remorse. He even looks at you with a smile of affected incredulity which only infuriates you further.

'Can you deny that you have done it?' you ask him again.

With assumed tranquillity he admits to being the agent of your sister's despair, adding, 'I rejoice in my success. Towards *him* I have been kinder than towards myself.'

His meaning does not escape you, though you refuse to show it.

'But it is not merely this affair,' you continue, 'on which my dislike is founded. Your character was unfolded in the recital which I received many months ago from Mr Wickham. On this subject, what can you have to say?'

'You take an eager interest in that gentleman's concerns,' says Darcy, in a less tranquil tone, and with a heightened colour.

'Who that knows what his misfortunes have been can help feeling an interest in him?' you continue. 'You have reduced him to his present state of poverty and deprived the best years of his life of an independence which was no less his due than his desert!'

'And this,' cries Darcy, as he walks with quick steps across the room, 'is your opinion of me! My faults, according to this calculation, are heavy indeed! But perhaps,' he adds, stopping in his walk, and turning towards you, 'these offences might have been overlooked, had not your pride been hurt by my honest confession of the scruples that had long prevented my forming any serious design. But disguise of every sort is my abhorrence. Could you expect me to rejoice in the inferiority of your connections? To congratulate myself on the hope of relations whose condition in life is so decidedly beneath my own?'

You are incensed, and feel yourself growing angrier by the moment. You try your utmost to speak with composure when you reply, saying, 'You are mistaken, Mr Darcy, if you suppose that the mode of your declaration affected me in any other way than as it spared me the concern which I might have felt in refusing you, had you behaved in a more gentlemanlike manner.'

You see him start at this. He says nothing, and you continue, 'You could not have made me the offer of your hand in any possible way that would have tempted me to accept it.'

'You have said quite enough, madam,' says Darcy, with forced civility. 'I perfectly comprehend your feelings, and have now only to be ashamed of what my own have been. Forgive me for having taken up so much of your time, and accept my best wishes for your health and happiness.'

And with these words he hastily leaves the room, his spirits clearly disturbed, and the next moment you hear him open the front door and quit the house.

The tumult of your mind is painfully great. Overwhelmed by feeling, you sit down and cry for half an hour. That you should receive an offer of marriage from Mr Darcy, that he should have been in love with you for so many months – so much in love as to wish to marry you in spite of all the objections which have made him prevent his friend's marrying your sister – is almost incredible! Despite yourself, you cannot help feeling that it is gratifying to have unconsciously inspired so strong an affection.

But his pride, his abominable pride, his shameless avowal of what he has done with respect to Jane, his unpardonable assurance in acknowledging his cruelty to Mr Wickham, soon overcomes the gratification momentarily excited by the consideration of his attachment. You continue in very agitating reflections till the sound of the Collinses returning hurries you away to your room.

You awake the next morning to the same thoughts and meditations which at length closed your eyes. You proceed directly to your favourite walk and after walking two or three times along the same part of the lane, Mr Darcy suddenly appears. 'I have been walking in the grove some time in the hope of meeting you,' says he, holding out a letter. 'Will you do me the honour of reading this?'

You take the letter, and with a slight bow, Darcy turns again into the plantation and is soon out of sight. It is dated from Rosings, at eight o'clock in the morning, and begins as follows:

Continue on page 136.

$\mathcal{T}$en days following the death of Mrs Churchill you receive a visit from Mrs Weston who tells you, in a state of great distress, that Frank Churchill is engaged to Miss Fairfax, and, what's more, that they have been engaged since last October, when they met at Weymouth. You had no idea that they had ever met before and almost jump with surprise. Mr Churchill has always been so disparaging of Miss Fairfax, and you wonder that you could have been so deceived. You think with horror of your conversations with Frank about Miss Fairfax and are deeply ashamed of what your behaviour has been.

Mr and Mrs Weston are both most anxious for you, believing that you are in love with Frank yourself, and it is with some difficulty that you are at last able to convince them that though you were at some time attached to Mr Frank Churchill, it has been many weeks since you have been able to think of him as anything but an amiable acquaintance. You wonder, however, how Miss Fairfax could have borne his attentions to you, and cannot but think ill of Frank for his behaviour towards you both.

You are worried for Maria, but when you call on her to give her the news you are surprised to discover that she has already heard it and does not appear to be in the least bit upset. You begin to wonder whether you have been mistaken in thinking her in love with Mr Churchill.

'I am pleased to see that you are not distressed by the news, Maria,' you say with a smile. 'I must confess that I thought you had formed an attachment to him yourself, and am pleased, in this case, to be proved wrong.'

'Me! In love with Mr Churchill!' she exclaims. 'How could you think such a thing? Never, never. I do not know who could ever look at him in the company of the *other* . . .'

It quickly becomes apparent that you were not mistaken in thinking her in love, only in the object of her affections. You are confused. If Maria has not been in love with Mr Churchill, then who *has* she been in love with? It is at this moment that a most distressing thought crosses your mind. You are suddenly struck with the awful possibility that she could mean Mr *Knightley*. It is suddenly absolutely necessary to have that thought contradicted.

'Maria!' you cry, before recollecting yourself. 'Let us understand each other now. Are you speaking of . . . Mr Knightley?'

You almost dread her response. When she tells you that she is indeed talking of Mr Knightley, and thought you knew, your worst fears are confirmed. You assure her that you most certainly did not. Maria is standing at one of the windows and you turn around to look at her in consternation.

'And have you any idea of Mr Knightley's returning your affection?' you ask with trepidation.

'Yes,' replies Maria modestly, but not fearfully, 'I must say that I have.'

Your eyes are instantly withdrawn; and you sit silently meditating, in a fixed attitude, for a few minutes. It darts through you suddenly, with the speed of an arrow, that you love Mr Knightley. A thousand feelings rush on you at once and from this moment you are wretched indeed. Only when threatened with his loss do you realise how much you love him.

Maria Lucas might think herself not unworthy of being exclusively and passionately loved by Mr Knightley, but *you* cannot. He has always been awake to your faults and has shown no scruples in pointing them out to you; no, Mr Knightley could never be in love with *you*.

The rest of the day, the following night, are hardly enough for your thoughts. You are bewildered amidst the confusion of all that has rushed on you within the last few hours. You sit still, you walk about, you try your own room, you try the shrubbery – in every place, every posture, you perceive that you have acted most weakly; that you have been imposed on by others in a most mortifying degree; that you have been imposing on yourself in a degree yet more mortifying; that you are wretched, and should probably find this day but the beginning of wretchedness.

The following day you take a walk about the garden to refresh your depressed spirits. You have only taken a few turns when you see Mr Knightley passing through the garden door and coming towards you. You did not even know he had returned from London. There is time only for the quickest arrangement of mind; you must be collected and calm. The 'How d'ye do's' are quiet and constrained on each side. You think he neither looks nor speaks cheerfully; and the first possible cause for it, suggested by your fears, is that he had perhaps communicated his plans to marry Maria to his brother while in London, and is pained by his unfavourable reaction.

You walk together. He is silent, and you cannot bear it long; something must be said. Trying to smile, you begin, 'You have some news to hear, now you are come back, that will rather surprise you.'

'Have I?' says he quietly, and looking at you. 'Of what nature?'

'The best nature in the world, Mr Knightley – a wedding,' you say, hinting at what you are sure is to pass between him and Maria.

After waiting a moment, as if to be sure you intend to say no more, he replies, 'If you mean Miss Fairfax and Frank Churchill, I have heard that already.'

'How is it possible?' you exclaim, turning your glowing cheeks towards him; for while you speak, it occurs to you that he might have called at the Lucases on his way.

'I had a few lines on parish business from Mr Weston this morning, and at the end of them he gave me a brief account of what had happened.'

You are quite relieved.

For a moment or two nothing is said. Suddenly you find your arm drawn within his, and pressed against his heart, and hear him thus saying, in a tone of great sensibility, speaking low, 'Time, my dearest Elizabeth, time will heal the wound.' Your arm is pressed again, as he continues in a more broken and subdued accent, and you just manage to catch the words '. . . Indignation . . . Abominable scoundrel!'

You understand him; he believes you in love with Mr Churchill and therefore imagines you to be suffering at the news of his engagement to Miss Fairfax. Such tender consideration cannot help but give you a flutter of pleasure.

As soon as you have recovered, you endeavour to assure him that you are not, and never have been, attached to Frank Churchill.

'My vanity was flattered, and I allowed his attentions, but I soon realised they were not serious. He has imposed on me, but he has not injured me. I have never been attached to him.'

You hope for an answer here – for a few words to say that your conduct was at least intelligible; but he is silent; and, as far as you can judge, deep in thought.

'He is a most fortunate man!' he suddenly exclaims with energy. 'He meets – at a common *watering place* – with an infinitely superior young woman, gains her affection, treats her negligently and conceals his engagement from his aunt. Then, when his aunt conveniently dies, he makes the engagement public and everyone is eager to promote his happiness. He has used everybody ill – and they are all delighted to forgive him. He is a fortunate man indeed!'

'You speak as if you envied him,' is your nervous reply, fearing every moment a declaration of his love for Maria.

'And I do envy him, Elizabeth. In one respect he is the object of my envy.'

You can say no more. You seem to be within half a sentence of Maria, and your immediate feeling is to avert the subject, if possible. Before you can speak, Mr Knightley startles you by saying, 'You will not ask me what is the point of envy. You are determined, I see, to have no curiosity. You are wise – but *I* cannot be wise. Elizabeth, I must tell what you will not ask, though I may wish it unsaid the next moment.'

You cannot bear to hear it.

'Then, don't speak it,' you exclaim eagerly. 'Take a little time, consider, do not commit yourself.'

'Thank you,' says he, in an accent of deep mortification, and not another syllable follows. You cannot bear to give him pain.

He wishes to confide in you – perhaps to consult you; cost you what it will, you will listen. You apologise for stopping him ungraciously and assure him that he can speak to you openly on any subject 'as a friend'.

'As a friend!' repeats Mr Knightley. 'Elizabeth, I fear that word. But I have gone too far already for concealment. Elizabeth, tell me, as a friend then, have I no chance of ever succeeding?'

He stops in his earnestness to look the question, and the expression of his eyes overpowers you. He entreats you to give him an answer at once, and say 'No' if it is to be said. You can really say nothing; you are overwhelmed with emotion at this most extraordinary and unexpected turn of events.

'I cannot make speeches, Elizabeth,' he resumes, and in a tone of sincere, decided and intelligible tenderness. 'If I loved you less, I might be able to talk about it more. But you know what I am. You hear nothing but truth from me. I have blamed you, and lectured you, and you have borne it as no other woman in England would have borne it. Bear with the truths I would tell you now, dearest Elizabeth, as well as you have borne with them. The manner, perhaps, may have as little to recommend them.'

You cannot help laughing as you remember with tender reflection the many, many times Mr Knightley has chastised you. And all the while he loved you! It is most extraordinary.

'God knows,' he continues, 'I have been a very indifferent lover. But you understand me. Yes, you see, you understand my feelings – and will return them if you can. At present, I ask only to hear, once to hear your voice.'

Mr Knightley is making you a proposal of marriage.

If you wish to accept the eligible Mr Knightley, turn to page 156.

If you wish to refuse him, suddenly doubting whether you could truly be happy with a man who might continue to 'blame' and 'lecture' you to the end of your days, turn to page 146.

*W*ith all the good grace you can manage in the circumstances, you accept Mr Darcy.

Mr Collins is shocked indeed to hear the news, and his first thought is of Lady Catherine. You know he will never forgive you for displeasing her but you comfort yourself with the knowledge that you'll soon be well settled and will not have to see Mr Collins above twice a year. If Mr Collins's shock is great, it is nothing next to that of your nearest relations. Jane is greatly fearful for your happiness, your father hardly less so, and your mother, for once, is entirely lost for words.

Your wedding is an intimate affair; with Darcy so offended by the inferiority of your connections, it could hardly be otherwise. After you have taken leave of your family in sombre spirits, you remove with your husband to Pemberley and settle into your new life.

Mr Darcy is civil to you when he is with you, but his duties on the estate are many, and frequently draw him from you. Not that you care much; it is a relief to be spared the necessity of making conversation. Mr Darcy has yet to learn how to converse with you on an easy footing and more often than not either inadvertently insults you, or is silent.

Without even the companionship of an affectionate husband to divert you, there is little for you to do at Pemberley. You are therefore forced to pass the long hours of the day reading your way through the many books in your extensive library, or walking about the estate and the surrounding countryside.

It is on one of these many walks, about a month after your marriage, that you meet the farmer responsible for the farm attached to Pemberley, a Mr Robert Martin. He is a very plain man, remarkably plain, but that is nothing compared with his entire want of gentility. At first it astonishes you that a man could be so very clownish, so totally without air, but as your acquaintance grows, you find yourself increasingly attracted to Mr Martin.

The situation at home shows no signs of improving and when Mr Darcy is not working, he spends more time reading than talking to you. Your resentment increases, and the more Mr Darcy neglects you, the less guilt you feel for seeking the society of Mr Martin. Your morning walks take you past his farm more frequently and your conversations grow longer. You are astonished and delighted to discover that not only is he literate, but he actually takes a keen interest in books. He even goes so far as to make you some recommendations, lending you *The Vicar of Wakefield*, for which you are most grateful, and which you are careful to conceal from the notice of your husband.

At last, unable to bear the stifling atmosphere at home any longer, you engage in a full and passionate affair with Mr Martin. It soon becomes public knowledge and you and Mr Martin are banished in disgrace, forever cut off from society, and are forced to spend the rest of your days in squalid lodgings in Portsmouth until the misery of your situation ruptures your love entirely and you hate each other with all the ardent passion with which you once loved.

THE END

Unfortunately, you have failed to complete your mission.

*Y*our appreciation of the picturesque is outstanding. You are entirely ready for a trip to the Lakes, and it is only a wonder that you have never been before.

Continue on page 108.

*B*e not alarmed, madam, on receiving this letter, by the apprehension of its containing any repetition of those sentiments or renewal of those offers which were last night so disgusting to you. You must pardon the freedom with which I demand your attention; your feelings, I know, will bestow it unwillingly, but I demand it of your justice.'

With no expectation of pleasure, but with the strongest curiosity, you read on.

'Two offences of a very different nature, and by no means of equal magnitude, you last night laid to my charge and I must endeavour now to explain my actions and motives.'

You learn that he had seen that Bingley preferred your sister but it was not till the Netherfield dance that he had had any apprehension of its being a serious attachment. He observed Bingley closely and could perceive that his partiality was beyond any that he had witnessed in him before, but though Jane received his attentions with pleasure, she did not seem to invite them by any participation of sentiment. He goes on to say that there were 'other causes of repugnance', and you smart at his use of the word.

Your mother's lineage, he writes, though objectionable, was nothing in comparison of that total want of propriety so frequently betrayed by her, by your flirtatious younger sisters, and occasionally even by your father. Miss Bingley's uneasiness, you learn, had been equally excited by the situation, and agreeing that no time should be lost, they joined Bingley in London. Darcy pointed out the evils of such a choice, described them earnestly, and assured him of Jane's indifference. Bingley's natural modesty meant it was easy for Darcy to convince him he had been deceived, and to persuade him against returning to Hertfordshire was the work of a moment. He has nothing more to say on the matter and no further apology to offer, and at this you find yourself shaking with indignation.

He then proceeds to defend himself against your second, more weighty accusation, of having injured Mr Wickham. Here, you are sure, he can have nothing to say to excuse his behaviour.

Mr Darcy's father supported Wickham through school, and afterwards at Cambridge, and had the highest opinion of him. After their fathers died, Wickham wrote to Darcy to ask for money in lieu of preferment since he had resolved against taking orders and had some idea of studying the law. Darcy rather wished than believed him to be sincere, but acceded to his proposal despite his reservation. Wickham resigned all claim to assistance in the Church in return for three thousand pounds. All connection between them seemed then to dissolve, and Darcy thought too ill of him to invite him to Pemberley.

Wickham lived in town, but law was just a pretence and being now free from restraint, his life was one of idleness and dissipation. After this period every appearance of acquaintance was dropped until last summer, when Wickham again most painfully obtruded on Darcy's notice.

Darcy's sister, who is ten years his junior, was taken from school a year ago to an establishment in London and last summer went with Mrs Younge, the woman who presided over it, to Ramsgate. Thither Mr Wickham also went, having learnt of their plans from Mrs Younge herself, with whom he had a prior acquaintance, and in whose character Darcy had been most unhappily deceived. By her connivance and aid he so far recommended himself to Georgiana that she believed herself in love and consented to an elopement. Mr Darcy joined them unexpectedly a day or two before the intended elopement, and she was unable to conceal it from him. Mr Wickham left the place immediately and Mrs Younge was removed from her charge. Mr Darcy invites you to consult Colonel Fitzwilliam if you need further testimony and concludes by saying:

'I will only add, God bless you. Fitzwilliam Darcy.'

You wish to discredit the letter entirely, and when you have gone through the whole, you put it hastily away, protesting that you will not regard it, that you will never look at it again. But it will not do: in half a minute the letter is unfolded again. The extravagance and general profligacy with which he charges Mr Wickham exceedingly shocks you; the more so, as you can bring no proof of its injustice. Of his former way of life nothing had been known in Hertfordshire but what he told himself. Aside from his affable company, you try to recollect some instance of goodness, some distinguished trait of integrity or benevolence, that might rescue him from the attacks of

Mr Darcy; but no such recollection befriends you.

You remember everything that passed between Wickham and yourself, in your conversation at Mr Philips's: he boasted of having no fear of seeing Mr Darcy – yet he avoided the Netherfield ball the very next week. You remember also that, before the Netherfield party had quitted the country, he told his story to no one but yourself; but that after their removal it was everywhere discussed.

Every lingering struggle in Wickham's favour grows fainter and fainter. Proud and repulsive though Mr Darcy's manners are, you have never, in the whole course of your acquaintance – an acquaintance which has latterly brought you much together – seen anything that betrayed him to be unprincipled or unjust – anything that spoke him of irreligious or immoral habits.

You grow absolutely ashamed of yourself. Of neither Darcy nor Wickham can you think without feeling that you have been blind, partial, prejudiced, absurd.

'How despicably have I acted!' you cry. 'I, who have prided myself on my discernment! I, who have valued myself on my abilities! How humiliating is this discovery! Yet, how just a humiliation! Had I been in love, I could not have been more wretchedly blind. But vanity, not love, has been my folly. Pleased with the preference of one, and offended by the neglect of the other, on the very beginning of our acquaintance, I have courted prepossession and ignorance, and driven reason away where either were concerned. Till this moment I never knew myself.'

After wandering along the lane for two hours, giving way to every variety of thought, fatigue, and a recollection of your long absence, make you at length return home.

*M*r Darcy and Colonel Fitzwilliam leave Rosings the very next morning. Until the time comes for you to leave Hunsford, you spend your days taking solitary walks in which you indulge in all the delight of unpleasant recollections.

At last you say your farewells and begin your journey, which will take you first to London for the night to collect Jane. You both arrive home at Longbourn in good time, and are greeted first by Kitty and Lydia, who delight in giving you news of the neighbourhood. You learn with some satisfaction that the militia are to leave Meryton in a fortnight.

'They are going to be encamped near Brighton,' says Lydia, 'and I do so want papa to take us all there for the summer! It would be such a delicious scheme, and I dare say would hardly cost anything at all. Mama would like to go, too, of all things! Only think what a miserable summer else we shall have!'

The thought of your entire family exposing itself to further ridicule and censure in Brighton is almost too much to bear. Your mother thinks it an excellent scheme; your father, thankfully, does not agree, though his answers are so vague and equivocal that your mother has not yet despaired of succeeding at last.

Your impatience to acquaint Jane with what has happened can no longer be overcome and, resolving to suppress every particular in which she is concerned, the next time you are alone you relate to her the chief of the scene between Mr Darcy and yourself. Her astonishment at his proposal and shock concerning what his letter had to tell of Wickham are great. Jane feels that it is your duty to make your knowledge public and expose Wickham as the fraud he really is. You are not so sure that is a good idea: Mr Darcy has not authorised you to make any of his communication public, and the details relating to his sister were meant to be kept as much as possible to yourself. You decide not to divulge Wickham's character to anyone else, and Jane at last is persuaded that there is no need to expose him since he will soon be gone from the neighbourhood. The tumult of your mind is allayed by this conversation, but still you dare not relate the other half of Mr Darcy's letter.

The first week of your return is soon gone and the second begins, announcing the last of the regiment's stay in Meryton. Lydia and Kitty regret it heartily, but the gloom of Lydia's prospect is shortly cleared away when she receives an invitation from Mrs Forster, the wife of the colonel of the regiment, to accompany her to Brighton. You consider the invitation the death warrant of all possibility of common sense for Lydia, and cannot help secretly advising your father not to let her go. Your father sees that your whole heart is in the subject, and affectionately takes your hand, and says in reply to your entreaty, 'My love, we shall have no peace at Longbourn if Lydia does not go to Brighton. Let her go, then. Colonel Forster is a sensible man, and will keep her out of any real mischief; and she is luckily too poor to be an object of prey to anybody.'

With this answer you are forced to be content, but your own opinion continues the same, and you leave him disappointed and sorry.

You see Mr Wickham one last time before he leaves Meryton. Upon his enquiry as to how you passed your time at Hunsford, you mention Colonel Fitzwilliam's and Mr Darcy's having both spent three weeks at Rosings. He asks you how you liked the Colonel and you can tell from his manner that he expects you to join him once again in an abuse of the Darcy family. You cannot be drawn in this time, however. Instead, you drop a hint to Wickham that suggests his lies have been exposed when you say, 'The Colonel's manners are very different from his cousin's, but I think Mr Darcy improves on acquaintance.'

Wickham's alarm appears in a heightened complexion and agitated look, and when you part it is with a mutual desire of never meeting again.

Lydia leaves for Brighton early the next morning and you rejoice over Wickham's and the militia's departure. Peace settles on Longbourn once again, and you resume your usual daily routines.

The following day you decide to take a walk.

To visit your aunt Philips in Meryton, turn to page 155.

To call on the Lucases, turn to page 147.

To his great surprise and disappointment, you refuse him. You tear yourself away from him as quickly as you can lest you should change your mind and give in to your heart's desire and make an extremely imprudent match.

Continue on page 91.

$\mathcal{Y}$ ou have an extremely basic appreciation of the picturesque. You are not really ready to look on the majestic beauty of the Lakes, but might be able to disguise it if you point admiringly to withered oaks and use adjectives such as 'bold' and 'rugged' from time to time.

Continue on page 108.

You refuse Mr Knightley and he is devastated. He gives up Donwell and goes to live in Antigua, though what he does there is anybody's guess; you never hear from him again.

No longer in his company, you forget Mr Knightley and turn your thoughts instead towards your forthcoming tour of the Lakes with your aunt and uncle Gardiner. You are more in need of 'rocks and mountains' now than you have ever been.

Continue on page 157.

You call on the Lucases and learn from them that one of your acquaintances is returning to the area tomorrow following a long spell abroad. After your recent trials, you could not be more delighted to hear it. Mr Knightley has been a friend to your family for many years and is greatly esteemed by your father, with whom he has spent many an evening playing backgammon. He is a firm favourite of *yours* too, and you are very pleased that he is returning now, when you are trying to forget Darcy's letter. Both handsome and agreeable, Mr Knightley more often than not has a cheerful manner and lively spirit, and though he is quick to remind you of your faults, you have learnt to bear it well, and respect his candour. Now that Charlotte is no longer at home, you feel that her sister, Maria, would also benefit from his society at this time, and having grown fond of her since the time you spent together at Hunsford, you promise to take her to visit Mr Knightley often.

Mr Knightley lives about a mile from Longbourn, and is the owner of a handsome estate by the name of Donwell Abbey. You visit him often, usually with Maria, and sometimes with Jane, too. You and Mr Knightley have much to discuss after such a long period of separation and you are grateful to have somebody with whom to talk over your present fears and anxieties over Lydia's holiday in Brighton. Mr Knightley expresses surprise that your father let her go, and is a little concerned himself, knowing what he does of Lydia's character, but he encourages you not to worry unduly about it. He turns the conversation towards happier subjects, and you both express your pleasure at the recent marriage between an old childhood friend of yours, Miss Taylor, and one of Mr Knightley's oldest acquaintances, Mr Weston. You agree to call on them together at the earliest opportunity.

The visit is made the following morning and you learn that they are expecting a visit from Mr Weston's son from a prior marriage, Mr Frank Churchill. You are confused as to why Mr Weston's son does not share his surname, but you learn that Frank has been raised by his wealthy uncle and aunt on his mother's side of the family, and since he is their heir, he has adopted their surname. Mrs Weston confesses to you that she is a little nervous about meeting him, and hopes she will be accepted. You are extremely curious to see him yourself, not least because Mr and Mrs Weston seem to have great hopes of the two of you getting along very well, and seem very anxious to make the introduction.

There is a great deal of excited talk of Frank Churchill in Meryton, and everyone seems eager for his appearance. Mr Knightley alone seems indifferent to the prospect of his arrival, and cannot understand why the whole neighbourhood should be so excited, or upon what evidence they are basing their opinion that he is such an 'impressive man of honour'.

'If I find him conversable,' says he one morning, 'I shall be glad of his acquaintance; but if he is only a chattering coxcomb, he will not occupy much of my time or thoughts.'

You are amused by Mr Knightley's tone, and accuse him, in good humour, of being prejudiced against Mr Churchill. You cannot imagine why he should be angry, and, finding it all very funny, you tease him about his prejudice against Mr Churchill from this time forward. It is only fair. Mr Knightley picks up on all *your* faults, after all.

After a delay which disappoints everyone except Mr Knightley, Mr Churchill at last arrives and the Westons call on you at Longbourn to make the introduction. You are sitting with Maria Lucas and Jane when they arrive and you are all extremely pleased to finally meet Mr Churchill. Your mother and other sisters are quick to join you when they hear who has come to visit, and you do not think too much has been said in his praise. He is a *very* good-looking gentleman and has an air of real elegance. His manner and address are good and you like him immediately. When he has gone, you are all generous in his praise.

'He is the most handsome man I ever saw in my life!' exclaims Maria.

Mr Churchill calls on you the next day and you accompany him and his stepmother on a tour of Meryton. He is warm and genuine in his praise of all that he sees, and after walking together so long, and thinking so much alike, you feel yourself so well acquainted with him, that you can hardly believe it to be only your second meeting. Mrs Weston sees it all with pleasure and more than once do you catch her smiling expressively as you and Mr Churchill converse.

*M*r Knightley's society brings you once more into contact with Mrs and Miss Bates. Mrs Bates is a very old lady, who lives modestly with her single daughter. Miss Bates boasts neither youth, beauty nor cleverness, and yet she is a happy woman, and a woman whom no one names without goodwill. You used to visit them frequently, but have lately been very remiss in your attentions. Following a lecture from Mr Knightley on your duties to those less fortunate than yourself, your conscience is pricked and you resolve to call on them with Jane and Maria the very next day.

You learn that Miss Bates is to receive a visit from her niece, Jane Fairfax, who was orphaned at a young age and subsequently taken into the care of a Colonel Campbell and his family. Miss Bates talks of Jane Fairfax almost as much as Mr Collins talks of Lady Catherine de Bourgh, and every letter from her is read by her aunt forty times over. You are very curious to see her, though after hearing so much in her praise, do not altogether look forward to the meeting with pleasure.

When Jane Fairfax appears you are forced to admit that she is both uncommonly handsome and very well accomplished, but upon getting to know her better you revert to your former dislike; you find her cold and reserved and you cannot forgive her for it. You are curious to know Mr Churchill's opinion of her and he is united with you in condemnation of her reserve, which cannot but please you. Mr Knightley seems to admire her greatly, however, and when you are slow to join him in his praise of her, he accuses you of being prejudiced against Miss Fairfax, just as you accused him of being prejudiced against Mr Churchill. You cannot help but laugh when it is represented to you in this way, but still you cannot teach yourself to like Miss Fairfax, despite your best efforts. Mr Knightley reproaches you for not paying your attentions to her as you ought, and reminds you that her situation is much less fortunate than your own – Miss Fairfax might have been raised as a gentleman's daughter, but no provisions were made for her adult life and consequently she will soon be forced to take work as a governess. In the light of this, you feel the justness of Mr Knightley's reproach and vow to be more attentive to Miss Fairfax.

From this time forward, you spend many evenings and days together with Frank Churchill and you both derive great pleasure from one another's company.

You are particularly pleased that he is always so ready to join you in criticising Miss Fairfax, and he assures you kindly one evening that though she is superior to you in her piano-playing, you definitely outshine her at dancing. You cannot entirely approve of his impropriety in saying it, but nevertheless such compliments cannot help but gratify your vanity.

You are just beginning to form a sincere and serious attachment to Mr Churchill, when Frank receives a letter from his uncle urging his return home on account of his aunt's having been taken extremely ill. You are sorely disappointed. Frank Churchill comes to take leave of you and seems on the point of confessing to you his love when he is most untimely interrupted by his father. Both gentlemen shortly take leave and you are very disappointed to see Mr Churchill go.

When he has departed, Jane, concerned for your happiness, wants to know the strength of your feelings for Mr Churchill.

'Well, Jane,' you reply with humour, 'from this sensation of listlessness, weariness, stupidity, this disinclination to sit down and employ myself, and this feeling of everything's being dull and insipid about the house, I can only conclude that I must be in love.'

Though you are joking, there is more than a little truth in what you say. Though you think of him a great deal just after he has gone, however, and form a thousand imaginary schemes for the progress and close of your attachment, the conclusion of every imaginary declaration on his side is that you refuse him. When you become aware of this, it strikes you that you cannot be very much in love after all.

Maria seems particularly melancholy following Mr Churchill's departure and you begin to wonder if she is not in love with him herself. Your suspicions are further aroused when during the course of some trivial discourse about marriage Maria says in a very serious tone, 'I shall never marry.' You look up at her and see her meaningful and troubled expression. It seems to you that Maria is indeed in love with Mr Churchill, but somehow considers him too superior for her.

'Is your resolution, or rather your expectation of never marrying, the result of an idea that the person whom you might prefer would be too greatly your superior to think of you?' you query her gently.

'Oh! Miss Elizabeth,' she cries. 'Believe me I have not the presumption to suppose – indeed I am not so mad. But it is a pleasure to me to admire him at a distance.'

You are touched by her modesty and resolve to praise her many merits when next in the company of Mr Churchill. Though he has never paid her any particular attention, and his wealthy aunt is very likely to object to the connection, you do not consider the case entirely hopeless. The greatest obstacle that stands in her way, as far as you see it, is that Mr Churchill is presently in love with *you*.

Before long Mr Churchill is able to return, owing to his aunt and uncle moving south to take advantage of the better weather. When he pays you his first visit, you perceive a change in his addresses: he has fallen out of love.

Continue on page 84.

You call on your aunt Philips, who talks of little but the departure of the militia and what a loss it is to the neighbourhood. You wish you had visited the Lucases.

The following weeks pass peacefully and uneventfully, and with little else to divert you, you turn your thoughts to your forthcoming tour to the Lakes.

Continue on page 157.

You marry Mr Knightley and remove to Donwell Abbey to settle into your new life. A short while after your wedding, you hear that Mr Darcy has married Miss Bingley and you feel a small pang of something like regret, though you chastise yourself for your foolish feelings. You put it from your mind as soon as possible and learn to be happy with Mr Knightley.

THE END

Congratulations. You have successfully completed your mission.

*Y*ou are only a fortnight from beginning your northern tour when a letter arrives from your aunt Gardiner, which at once delays its commencement and curtails its extent. Mr Gardiner's business obliges you to give up the Lakes and go no further northward than Derbyshire. The mention of Derbyshire brings forward many thoughts; it is impossible for you to see the word without thinking of Pemberley and its owner, Mr Darcy, whom you haven't seen since he gave you his most affecting letter at Rosings.

At length Mr and Mrs Gardiner appear at Longbourn and you set off the following morning in pursuit of novelty and amusement. You head first to the little town of Lambton, the site of Mrs Gardiner's former residence, which your aunt tells you is just five miles from Pemberley. Mrs Gardiner expresses an inclination to see Pemberley again and you are applied to for your approbation. You are distressed. The possibility of meeting Mr Darcy while viewing the place instantly occurs and you blush at the very idea. It would be truly dreadful and you think it better to speak openly to your aunt than to run such a risk. Understanding your concern, Mrs Gardiner asks the chambermaid whether the family is down for the summer, and a most welcome negative follows.

With your fears allayed, you are at leisure to admit to yourself that you are indeed curious to see the house. You have heard stories connected to the place from both Darcy and Wickham, and, moreover, cannot help wondering what kind of establishment Mr Darcy keeps. When the subject is revived you can readily say, with a proper air of indifference, that you have not really any dislike to the scheme.

To Pemberley, therefore, you are to go.

Congratulations. You have completed Volume Two.

Though temptations on every side have been great, your choices have led you closer to making a prudent and truly equal match.

Proceed to Volume Three on page 159.

VOLUME THREE

As you drive along, you watch for the first appearance of Pemberley with some perturbation; and when at length you arrive at the gate, your spirits are in a high flutter. You drive for some time through a beautiful wood stretching over a wide extent and you silently admire every remarkable spot and point of view. You soon see the house itself on the opposite side of a valley. It is a large, handsome stone building, standing well on rising ground, and backed by a ridge of high woody hills. You are delighted. You have never seen a place for which nature has done more, or where natural beauty has been so little counteracted by an awkward taste for artificial 'improvements'. After the pomp and honour of Rosings, you had rather expected to find Darcy's family pride reflected in the grounds of Pemberley, and are forced to admit that you have underestimated Mr Darcy.

On applying to see the house, you are admitted into the hall, where you are met by the housekeeper, Mrs Reynolds. She is a respectable-looking elderly woman, and again, is much less fine, and more civil, than you had expected. You follow her through the door to the dining parlour and find a large, well-proportioned room, handsomely fitted up. You go to a window to enjoy its prospect: every disposition of the ground is good; and you look on the whole scene – the river, the trees scattered on its banks, and the winding of the valley, as far as you can trace it – with delight.

'And of this place,' you think, 'I might have been mistress! Instead of viewing these rooms as a stranger, I might have rejoiced in them as my own, and welcomed to them as visitors my uncle and aunt. But no' – you recollect yourself, remembering Darcy's scruples concerning the 'inferiority of your connections' – 'that could never be: my uncle and aunt would have been lost to me; I should not have been allowed to invite them.'

This is a lucky recollection – it saves you from something like regret.

You learn from Mrs Reynolds that Mr Darcy is expected tomorrow with a large party of friends and you rejoice that your own journey was not by any circumstance delayed a day. You pass through other rooms and Mrs Reynolds draws your attention to a likeness of Mr Darcy suspended amongst several other miniatures, over a mantelpiece.

'It is a handsome face,' says Mrs Gardiner, looking at the picture, 'but, Lizzy, you can tell us whether it is like or not.'

Mrs Reynolds's respect for you seems to increase on this intimation of your knowing her master.

'Does the young lady know Mr Darcy?' she asks.

You colour, and say, 'A little.'

'And do not you think him a very handsome gentleman, ma'am?'

'Yes, very handsome,' you reply.

'And he is such a good master,' she continues. 'I have never had a cross word from him in my life, and I have known him ever since he was four years old.'

That he is not a good-tempered man has been your firmest opinion, and you are extremely surprised to hear her say otherwise. She goes on to say that it is no surprise to her that he has grown up so good-natured, since he was the 'sweetest-tempered, most generous-hearted boy in the world'.

You almost stare at her. 'Can this be Mr Darcy!' you think. You listen, wonder, doubt, and are impatient for more.

'He is the best landlord, and the best master,' she continues, 'that ever lived; not like the wild young men nowadays, who think of nothing but themselves.'

With a pang, you remember Mr Wickham.

'Some people call him proud,' she continues, 'but I am sure I never saw anything of it. To my fancy, it is only because he does not rattle away like other young men.'

'In what an amiable light does this place him!' you think, amazed and astonished by Mrs Reynolds's account. Everything you have heard is contrary to what you had expected; everything is contrary to your own opinions of him.

'This fine account of him,' whispers your aunt as you walk on, 'is not quite consistent with his behaviour to our poor friend, Mr Wickham.'

'Perhaps we might be deceived,' you caution her.

'That is not very likely; our authority was too good.'

You earnestly wish to put her right, but judge that now is not that time.

On reaching the spacious lobby above, you are shown into the picture gallery. There are many family portraits, and you walk on in quest of the only face whose features are known to you. At last it arrests you – and you behold a striking resemblance to Mr Darcy, with such a smile over the face as you remember to have sometimes seen when he looked at you.

You stand several minutes before the picture in earnest contemplation. At this moment, in your mind, there is a more gentle sensation towards the original than you have ever felt in the height of your acquaintance. What praise is more valuable than the praise of an intelligent servant? As a brother, a landlord, a master, you consider how many people's happiness are in his guardianship. As you stand before the canvas, you think of the regard he has shown you with a deeper sentiment of gratitude than ever before.

When all of the house that is open to general inspection has been seen, you return downstairs, and taking leave of the housekeeper, are consigned over to the gardener. He asks you which part of the grounds you would like to see first.

To take the path across the park to the handsome woodland first, turn to page 215.

To go to the river first, turn to page 197.

You accept the Philipses' invitation and journey to Bath. You learn that your distant cousins Mary and Charles Musgrove are also in Bath for the season and your aunt Philips encourages you to call on them as soon as possible in the hope that a change of company will help to lift your spirits. You think it a scheme unlikely to succeed, but since you have precious few other acquaintances in Bath, you acquiesce and call on the Musgroves.

Mary Musgrove is far from beautiful and has none of the Bennet family understanding or temper, but she has a good heart. Her husband Charles does nothing with much zeal except sport, but is civil and agreeable. Charles's attractive but somewhat frivolous sister Louisa is also staying with them for a short while, and though their values are on the whole a little too superficial for your liking, you feel that the Musgroves could be a welcome distraction from your unpleasant reflections on Lydia and Wickham's marriage, and Darcy's part in it. You have not yet learnt to put from your mind the idea that he did it all for you, but you know it is hardly possible. You therefore vow to forget Mr Darcy and engage wholeheartedly in life at Bath. Time, you hope, will come to heal that particular wound.

After the usual enquiries have been made, Louisa proposes a walk to visit the Pump Room and you all readily agree. You have not been there long when Charles begs leave to introduce you to an old friend of his from the navy, by the name of Captain Wentworth. You instantly start, and a deep crimson blush overspreads your features. The gentleman is scarcely more composed and the Musgroves are surprised indeed. They all begin their enquiries and all long to know the meaning of this extraordinary reaction!

'We were acquainted once,' is all the gentleman replies, and you are just able to nod in agreement before hastily making your excuses and leaving the room in search of fresh air.

You have indeed met Captain Wentworth before, and in fact were most intimately acquainted with him just three years ago after meeting him in London with your aunt and uncle Gardiner. Mr Wentworth was a remarkably fine young man, with a great deal of intelligence, spirit and brilliancy, and both of you soon fell deeply in love. He proposed and you most happily accepted. Your happiness was but short, however. He had no fortune and no hopes of attaining one but in the most precarious profession of the navy, and Mrs Gardiner strongly objected. Always having had great respect for your aunt's opinion, you were persuaded to believe the engagement a wrong thing and to call it off. You do not blame your aunt for what she did, but you have often wondered whether you might not have been happier with him, no matter what the difficulties, than you have been in sacrificing him.

*S*eeing Captain Wentworth again so unexpectedly has thrown your mind into great turmoil. When you vowed to put Mr Darcy from your mind, little did you expect to be visited by this ghost from your past! As your feelings for Mr Darcy have grown over these past weeks, the memory of your attachment to Captain Wentworth has been always at the back of your mind. You had endeavoured to forget him, but only because you were certain you would never see each other again. Now, however, you are thrown into a state of great confusion.

From this time you and Captain Wentworth are repeatedly in the same circle owing to his friendship with your cousin Charles. You have no conversation together, however, and no intercourse but what the commonest civility requires. You know not what to think, and long to know what he feels for you now. You are soon spared all suspense when Mary reveals to you that Captain Wentworth said he considers you 'so altered he should not have known you again'.

You cannot entirely blame him. You rejected him in the belief that you were acting in his best interests, but it would seem that you sacrificed his happiness along with your own, and you cannot escape the thought that it might, perhaps, have been all for nothing. His cold civility cuts you to the quick, and it is with great difficulty that you maintain your characteristic good humour in the situation. To add to your difficulties, it quickly becomes apparent that Louisa Musgrove greatly admires the Captain, and worse still, that the admiration is reciprocated. They are always

— **167** —

together, and always gay. You cannot help but be a little surprised that Wentworth should be attracted to a girl as frivolous and flighty as Louisa; her character is so different from your own. He was always wont to value good sense above all else, but time perhaps has changed his tastes.

You do your best to be civil and polite to Captain Wentworth, and avoid being in his company more often than necessary by spending more time with your uncle and aunt Philips. You cannot avoid him entirely, however, and since your cousins know nothing of your history, it is difficult always to find excuses not to see them when they are with the Captain. On one such occasion you are unlucky enough to overhear a conversation between him and Louisa in which she is recounting a recent moment of resistance against a relative's attempted interference in her plans. Although you do not know the details, you hear enough to make you stop.

'What!' she exclaims, 'would I be turned back from doing a thing that I had determined to do, and that I knew to be right, by the airs and interference of such a person, or of any person I may say? No, I have no idea of being so easily persuaded. When I have made up my mind, I have made it.'

'*Yours* is the character of decision and firmness, I see,' he replies. 'It is the worst evil of too yielding and indecisive a character, that no influence over it can be depended on. You are never sure of a good impression being durable; everybody may sway it. Let those who would be happy be firm.'

The sounds retreat and you hear no more, but your own emotions keep you fixed. Though his words were not directed at you, and he cannot know you heard him, in the light of your aunt's influence in persuading you against him, it can be without question what the Captain thinks of *your* character.

A few days later, Captain Wentworth proposes a trip to the seaside town of Lyme, to visit an old friend by the name of Captain Harville. Everyone is wild to go, and will not think of going without you. You have little choice; you must submit to the plan, though you foresee little pleasure in being witness to the unfolding romance between Louisa and Wentworth.

You all set off at the appointed time and arrive at Lyme earlier than expected. After securing accommodations, and ordering a dinner at the inn, you all walk directly down to the sea. Captain Wentworth calls on his friends the Harvilles, while you and the rest of the party walk on towards the famous harbour wall, the Cobb, where Wentworth will join you. He soon arrives with Captain and Mrs Harville, and a Captain Benwick, who is staying with them. Captain Harville is tall and fair; and his manner open and agreeable. His wife is plain, but warm and unaffected. Their friend Captain Benwick is shorter than

Captain Harville but is perhaps more handsome, and his dark features become him well.

The next morning, before breakfast, you take a walk down to the sea with the rest of your party. As you are ascending the steps back up from the beach you pass a gentleman who politely draws back to let you by. As you pass he looks at you with a degree of earnest admiration which you cannot be insensible of. You are looking remarkably well, it is true; the sea air has done you a world of good. It is evident that the gentleman admires you exceedingly and Captain Wentworth looks round at you instantly in a way which suggests that he has seen the look the gentleman has given you, and that just for this moment, he too thinks you worthy of admiration. You cannot help wondering if he thinks you 'so altered he would not have known you' *now*.

You return to the inn in high spirits. You have nearly done breakfast, when the sound of a carriage draws half the party to the window. The owner of the curricle is the same man you met this morning, who is at this very moment taking leave of the inn. You learn from the waiter that his name is Mr Bennet, a gentleman of large fortune, on his way to Bath.

'Bennet! Bless me!' cries Mary, 'It must be our cousin; it must be our Mr Bennet, it must, indeed! How very extraordinary! In the very same inn with us! Lizzy, must not it be our Mr Bennet?'

Mr Bennet is from a branch of your family that your father did not get on well with, and a family quarrel has cut off this Mr Bennet from your notice. You all wonder at the coincidence of meeting him here.

Soon after breakfast the handsome Captain Benwick joins you again, to take a walk about Lyme. After exploring the town you all walk to the Cobb, but there is too much wind to make the high part pleasant, and you all agree to get down the steps to the lower. Everyone is content to pass quietly and carefully down the steep flight, excepting Louisa: she must be jumped down them by Captain Wentworth. You find her impulsiveness petulant, though Captain Wentworth seems to find it charming.

You wonder at him for indulging her in such a dangerous game, but it seems there is nothing he will not do to make her happy. She is safely down, and instantly to show her enjoyment, runs up the steps to be jumped down again. He advises her against it, thinks the jar too great; but she smiles and says, 'I am determined I will.' He puts out his hands; she is too precipitate by half a second, she falls on the pavement on the Lower Cobb, and is taken up lifeless!

There is no wound, no blood, no visible bruise; but her eyes are closed, she breathes not, her face is like death. Captain Wentworth catches her up, kneels with her in his arms and looks on her with a face as pallid as her own, in an agony of silence.

'She is dead! She is dead!' screams Mary.

Continue on page 206.

About this time, your mother's mind is opened again to the agitation of hope, by an article of news which has now begun to circulate: the housekeeper at Netherfield has received orders to prepare for the arrival of her master, who is coming down in a day or two to shoot there for several weeks. Jane is unable to hear of Bingley's coming without changing colour, though she assures you later that she has long since given up all feelings of attachment to him.

Mr Bingley comes at last, and on the third morning after his arrival in Hertfordshire, your mother spies him from her dressing-room window entering the paddock and riding towards the house – with Mr Darcy. Your astonishment at Darcy's coming – at his coming to Netherfield, to Longbourn, and voluntarily seeking you again even though Lydia is now married, at Darcy's own expense, to his greatest enemy, Mr Wickham – is almost equal to what you had known on first witnessing his altered behaviour in Derbyshire.

You sit intently at work, striving to be composed, and not daring to lift up your eyes. On the gentlemen's appearing, Jane's colour increases; yet she receives them with tolerable ease. You say as little to either as civility allows, and sit down again to your work with an eagerness which it does not often command.

You venture only one glance at Darcy. He looks serious, as usual, and, you think, more as he used to look in Hertfordshire than as you saw him at Pemberley; more reserve, and less anxiety to please than when you last met are plainly expressed. You are disappointed, and angry with yourself for being so.

'Could I expect it to be otherwise!' you say to yourself. 'Yet why did he come?'

Your mother is extremely civil to Mr Bingley and, to your great shame, pointedly cold towards Mr Darcy. She gloats over the marriage of Lydia but laments that she must live so far away, and you are in agonies at your mother's rudeness.

When the gentlemen rise to go away, your mother invites Mr Bingley to come the next morning to shoot with your father. He assents, and leaves with Mr Darcy.

*B*ingley is punctual to his appointment and after the shooting, returns to dinner. His attentions to Jane give you great pleasure and he seems, if possible, more in love with her than he was when he was last at Netherfield. That evening you have a letter to write and go into the breakfast room for that purpose soon after tea. On returning to the drawing room when your letter is finished, you see, to your infinite surprise, your sister and Bingley standing together over the hearth as if engaged in earnest conversation. Had this led to no suspicion, the faces of both, as they hastily turn round and move away from each other, would have told it all. Not a syllable is uttered by either; and you are on the point of going away again when Bingley, whispering a few words to your sister, runs out of the room.

Instantly embracing you, Jane acknowledges with the liveliest emotion that she is the happiest creature in the world.

'Oh! Lizzy, why am I thus singled from my family, and blessed above them all! If I could but see *you* as happy! If there *were* but such another man for you!'

She goes instantly to your mother, and you are left to smile at the rapidity and ease with which an affair that has given you so many months of suspense and vexation is finally settled.

One morning, about a week after Bingley's engagement to Jane, you receive a very unexpected visitor in the name of Lady Catherine de Bourgh. Your astonishment is beyond words.

She enters the room with an air more than usually ungracious, makes no other reply to your salutation than a slight inclination of the head, and sits down without saying a word. Your mother, with great civility, begs her Ladyship to take some refreshment; but Lady Catherine very resolutely, and not very politely, declines to eat anything; and then, rising up, asks you to show her the little copse on the other side of your lawn.

You obey, and as soon as you enter the copse, Lady Catherine begins by declaring that you can be at no loss to understand the reason of her journey. You reply, with unaffected astonishment, that you have not the least idea why she has paid you the honour of visiting, and from her furious expression you quickly see that this was not the answer she wanted to hear.

'A report of a most alarming nature reached me two days ago,' she says in an angry tone. 'I was told that not only was your sister on the point of being most advantageously married, but that *you,* that Miss Elizabeth Bennet, would in all likelihood be soon afterwards united to my nephew Mr Darcy.'

You are once again genuinely astonished. You know not what to think and your spirits are thrown into discomposure.

'Though I *know* it must be a scandalous falsehood . . .' continues Lady Catherine, 'I instantly resolved on setting off for this place, that I might make my sentiments known to you.'

Your nerves are greatly agitated, both by Lady Catherine's tone, and the idea that such a report could be in existence at all. Who could have started it? Could it have in some way come from Darcy himself? You can scarcely allow yourself to consider it a possibility and instantly banish the thought from your mind.

You direct your attention back to Lady Catherine and tell her that her coming to Longbourn will only be a confirmation of the report if, indeed, such a report exists.

'This is not to be borne!' cries Lady Catherine.

She asks you directly if you are engaged to him, and though you would rather not, for the mere purpose of obliging Lady Catherine, answer this question, you cannot but say after a moment's deliberation, 'I am not.'

'And will you promise me never to enter into such an engagement?' she asks.

You will make her no promise of the kind and tell her that she has widely mistaken your character if she thinks you can be worked on by such persuasions as hers. You beg, therefore, to be importuned no further on the subject, and turn back towards the house.

'Not so hasty, if you please,' she insists, stopping you before you can get away. 'I have by no means done, I have still another objection to add. I am no stranger to the particulars of your youngest sister's infamous elopement and patched-up marriage. Is *such* a girl to be my nephew's sister? Heaven and earth – are the shades of Pemberley to be thus polluted?'

You know that Lydia's elopement has ruined, forever, any hope of a renewal of Darcy's attentions to you, and you do not need to be reminded of it by Lady Catherine.

'You can *now* have nothing further to say,' you resentfully answer. 'You have insulted me in every possible method; I must beg to return to the house. I have nothing further to say; you know my sentiments.'

You reach the door of her carriage, when, turning hastily

round, Lady Catherine concludes, 'I take no leave of you, Miss Bennet. I send no compliments to your mother. You deserve no such attention. I am most seriously displeased.'

You make no answer, and, without attempting to persuade her Ladyship to return to the house, walk quietly into it yourself.

The discomposure of spirits which this extraordinary visit throws you into cannot be easily overcome, and it is many hours before you can think of it less than incessantly. From what the report of your engagement can originate, you are at a loss to imagine, except perhaps the fact that the marriage of Jane and Bingley will bring you and Darcy more frequently together.

A few days after Lady Catherine's visit, Mr Bingley once again brings Mr Darcy with him to Longbourn. The gentlemen arrive early; and before your mother has time to tell Mr Darcy of your having seen his aunt – of which you sit in momentary dread – Bingley, who wants to be alone with Jane, proposes your all walking out. It is immediately agreed to, to your own great relief: your mother is not in the habit of walking and will therefore have no further opportunity to embarrass you. Your sister Mary can never spare time for walking, but Kitty declares herself willing and the remaining five of you set off together. Bingley and Jane soon allow the rest of you to outstrip them and lag behind, while you, Kitty and Darcy are left to entertain each other. Very little is said by any of you: Kitty is too much afraid of him to talk; you are secretly forming a desperate resolution to thank him for what he did for Lydia; and what Darcy's own reasons for silence are you dread to think.

Kitty wishes to call on Maria and so the three of you walk in the direction of Lucas Lodge. As you see no occasion for making it a general concern, when Kitty leaves, you go boldly on with Darcy alone. Now is the moment for your resolution to be executed and, while your courage is high, you thank him for his unexampled kindness to your poor sister.

'I am sorry, exceedingly sorry,' replies Darcy, in a tone of surprise and emotion, 'that you have ever been informed of what may, in a mistaken light, have given you uneasiness.'

You thank him again and again, in the name of all your family, for his generous compassion.

'If you will thank me,' he replies, 'let it be for yourself alone. I shall not attempt to deny that the wish of giving you happiness added to my other inducements to act. But your family owes me nothing. Much as I respect them, I believe I thought only of you.'

You are so very surprised at this unexpected turn of events, and so overwhelmed with emotion by what you have heard, that for some moments you are too embarrassed to say a word. After a short pause, your companion adds, 'You are too generous to trifle with me. If your feelings are still what they were last April, tell me so at once. My affections and wishes are unchanged; but one word from you will silence me on this subject forever.'

Feeling all the more than common awkwardness and anxiety of his situation, you are now forced to speak yourself; and immediately, though not very fluently, give him to understand that your sentiments have undergone so material a change since the period to which he alludes, as to make you receive with gratitude and pleasure his present assurances. You can barely meet his eye, but when you do, you see that the expression of heartfelt delight which diffuses his face becomes him exceedingly well. You listen in a quiet ecstasy as he tells you of feelings which, in proving of what importance you are to him, make his affection every moment more valuable.

You walk on, without knowing in what direction. There is too much to be thought, and felt, and said, for attention to any other objects. You talk over every past misunderstanding and the circumstances which led to your respective changes in opinion of each other and walk together happily till the time calls you back indoors.

The news shocks your family greatly. Jane is worried that you do not really love him, your mother is delighted at how rich you'll be, and your father is incredulous. At length, by repeated assurances that Mr Darcy is really the object of your choice, and by explaining the gradual change which your estimation of him has undergone, relating your absolute certainty that his affection is not the work of a day, but has stood the test of many months' suspense, you conquer your father's incredulity, and reconcile him to the match. You retire to bed that evening perhaps even more happy than Jane, and soon fall into a deep and blissful sleep.

It is a great surprise to you therefore when you wake suddenly in the middle of the night, your heart beating at your chest and a cold sweat on your brow. You feel a deep knot of anxiety within you. What could possibly be wrong? The man you love wants to marry you and nothing stands in your way. Just hours before, you were the happiest woman alive; now you feel sick with worry. There is something troubling you, but you know not what it could be. A bad dream perhaps? All you have is an impression of a feeling, a deep uneasiness that you cannot immediately explain.

If you decide to ignore this uneasy feeling, turn to page 218.

If you decide to get out of bed and examine your feelings more closely, turn to page 220.

*D*esiring news from your sister, you were a good deal disappointed in not finding a letter from Jane on your first arrival at Lambton; and this disappointment has been renewed on each of the mornings since; but on the third morning you receive two letters at once, the first one marked as having been mis-sent elsewhere.

You had just been preparing to walk as the letters came in; and your uncle and aunt, leaving you to enjoy them in quiet, set off by themselves. The one mis-sent must be first attended to; it was written five days ago. Nothing could have prepared you for what you now read: your fifteen-year-old sister Lydia has eloped with Wickham. Worse still, the second letter reveals that there is reason to fear she and Wickham are not gone to Gretna Green to be married. Lydia's short letter to Mrs Forster, with whom she was staying in Brighton, gave them to understand that they were going to Gretna Green, but something was dropped by Wickham's friend and your acquaintance, the officer Denny, expressing his belief that Wickham never intended to go there, or to marry Lydia at all. Colonel Forster, taking the alarm, set off from Brighton, intending to follow their route, but could trace them no further than Clapham.

Jane begs you all to go to Longbourn as soon as possible; your father is going to London with Colonel Forster instantly but your uncle's advice and assistance are longed for.

'Oh! Where, where is my uncle?' you cry, darting from your seat, but as you reach the door it is opened by a servant, and Mr Darcy appears. Your pale face and impetuous manner make him start, and before he can recover himself enough to speak, you hastily exclaim, 'I beg your pardon, but I must leave you. I must find Mr Gardiner this moment, on business that cannot be delayed; I have not an instant to lose.'

'Good God! What is the matter?' he cries, with more feeling than politeness; then recollecting himself, 'I will not detain you a minute; but let me, or the servant, go after Mr and Mrs Gardiner. You are not well enough; you cannot go yourself.'

His kindness only makes the moment worse. You hesitate, but your knees tremble under you, and you feel how little would be gained by your attempting to pursue the Gardiners. Calling back the servant, therefore, you commission him, though in so breathless an accent as makes you almost unintelligible, to fetch his master and mistress home instantly.

On his quitting the room you sit down, unable to support yourself, and looking so miserably ill that Darcy says, in a tone of gentleness and commiseration, 'Let me call your maid. Is there nothing you could take to give you present relief? A glass of wine – shall I get you one? You are very ill.'

'No, I thank you,' you reply, endeavouring to recover yourself. 'There is nothing the matter with me. I am quite well. I am only distressed by some dreadful news I have just received from Longbourn.'

You burst into tears as you allude to it, and for a few minutes cannot speak another word. At length you speak again. 'I have just had a letter from Jane, with such dreadful news. It cannot be concealed from anyone. My youngest sister has left all her friends – has eloped; has thrown herself into the power of . . . of Mr Wickham. They are gone off together from Brighton. *You* know him too well to doubt the rest. She has no money, no connections, nothing that can tempt him to . . . She is lost forever.'

Darcy is fixed in astonishment. You earnestly regret him knowing.

'But is it certain – absolutely certain?' he asks.

'Oh yes! They left Brighton together on Sunday night, and were traced almost to London, but not beyond: they are certainly not gone to Gretna Green.'

'And what has been done, what has been attempted, to recover her?'

'My father is gone to London, and Jane has written to beg my uncle's immediate assistance; and we shall be off, I hope, in half an hour. But nothing can be done – I know very well that nothing can be done. How is such a man to be worked on? How are they even to be discovered? I have not the smallest hope. It is in every way horrible!'

Darcy seems scarcely to hear you, and is walking up and down the room in earnest meditation, his brow contracted, his air gloomy. At this moment you understand your own wishes for the first time; and never have you so honestly felt that you could have loved him, as now, when all love must be in vain.

Mr Darcy fears you have long been desiring his absence and wishes there were something he could do or say to offer consolation. He again expresses his sorrow for your distress, wishes it a happier conclusion than there is at present reason to hope, and after leaving his compliments for your relations, with only one serious, parting look, goes away.

Mr and Mrs Gardiner hurry back in alarm, and after the first exclamations of surprise and horror, Mr Gardiner readily promises every assistance in his power. You set off for Longbourn as soon as possible and, sleeping one night on the road, reach Longbourn by dinnertime the next day. There is little to learn from Jane: your father is in town but will not write till he has something of importance to mention; your mother refuses to leave her dressing room. Jane shows you Lydia's letter, which is thoughtless and vain but does at least show that *she* believed they were going to Gretna Green to be married.

Your whole party is in hopes of a letter from Mr Bennet the next morning, but the post comes in without bringing a single line from him. Mr Gardiner waits only for the letters before he sets off for London. Every day at Longbourn is now a day of anxiety; but the most anxious part of each is when the post is expected. Through letters, whatever of good or bad is to be told will be communicated, and every succeeding day is expected to bring some news of importance.

Mr Gardiner writes with information he has learnt from corresponding with Colonel Forster, but it is not good. It transpires that Wickham left gaming debts behind him to a very considerable amount, and Colonel Forster believes that more than a thousand pounds will be necessary to clear his expenses at Brighton. He owes a good deal to the merchants and tavern keepers in the town, but his debts of honour to his friends there are still more formidable.

Rendered spiritless by the ill-success of all their endeavours, Mr Bennet yields to his brother-in-law's entreaty that he return to his family, and leaves it to him to continue their pursuit. Two days after Mr Bennet's return an express comes for him from Mr Gardiner. He has seen them both; they are not married, nor can he find there was any intention of being so; but if Mr Bennet is willing to assure to Lydia, by settlement, her equal share of the five thousand pounds secured among you all after his death and enter into an engagement of allowing her, during his life, one hundred pounds per annum, and fifty a year after he is gone, they will very soon be married.

'They must marry,' says Mr Bennet. 'There is nothing else to be done. But there are two things that I want very much to know: one is, how much money your uncle has laid down, to bring it about; and the other, how I am ever to pay him. No man in his senses would marry Lydia on so slight a pecuniary temptation. Wickham's a fool if he takes her with a farthing less than ten thousand pounds.'

Shame for your sister's actions once again overcomes you. Mrs Bennet can hardly contain herself for joy, and in vain do you remind her what an obligation your uncle's actions have put you all under.

You are now most heartily sorry that from the distress of the moment, you were led to make Mr Darcy acquainted with your fears for your sister; for since her marriage will so shortly give the proper termination to the elopement, you might hope to conceal its unfavourable beginning from all those who were not immediately aware. It is not to be supposed that Mr Darcy will connect himself with a family where, to every other objection, will now be added an alliance and relationship of the nearest kind with the man whom he so justly scorns.

You begin now to comprehend that he is exactly the man who, in disposition and talents, would most suit you. It was a union that would be to the advantage of both; by your ease and liveliness, his mind might be softened, his manners improved; and from his judgement, information and knowledge of the world, you must receive benefit of greater importance. But no such happy marriage can now teach the admiring multitude what connubial felicity really is.

Mr Gardiner soon writes again to say that Mr Wickham has resolved on quitting the militia in favour of the Regulars. He has the promise of an ensigncy in General —'s regiment, now quartered in the north.

The wedding day arrives. The carriage is sent to meet

the newly-weds, and they are at Longbourn by dinner-time. Their arrival is greeted with rapture by your mother, who throws her arms around Lydia and fawns over her new son-in-law.

*O*ne morning, soon after their arrival, as she is sitting with you and Jane, Lydia gives you an account of every moment leading up to her wedding. You think that there cannot be too little said on the subject but she insists on giving you every detail. It is as she does so that she lets slip that Mr Darcy was present and had attended Mr Wickham. You are utterly amazed.

'But gracious me!' exclaims Lydia, 'I quite forgot! I ought not to have said a word about it. I promised them so faithfully! What will Wickham say? It was to be such a secret!'

'If it was to be secret,' says Jane, 'say not another word on the subject. You may depend upon my seeking no further.'

Just for this moment, you wish Jane were not always so uncompromisingly virtuous.

'Oh! Certainly,' you add, though burning with curiosity, 'we will ask you no questions.'

Conjectures as to the meaning of Mr Darcy's being at your sister's wedding, rapid and wild, hurry into your brain; but you are satisfied with none. You cannot bear such suspense; hastily seizing a sheet of paper, you write a short letter to your aunt to request an explanation of the intelligence Lydia has dropped.

You receive an answer very quickly. She is greatly surprised that you do not already know the details. Not long after your uncle had arrived in London to help in the search for your sister he received a visit from Mr Darcy, who had found out where Lydia and Wickham were. He had left Derbyshire the day after you did to find them out, blaming himself for not making Wickham's true character publicly known. He had called it, therefore, his duty to step forward, and endeavour to remedy an evil which had been brought on by himself.

He discovered them through a Mrs Younge, who was some time ago governess to Miss Darcy, and was dismissed from her charge following Miss Darcy's own scrape with Wickham. He tried to persuade Lydia to quit her present disgraceful situation and return to her friends as soon as they could be prevailed on to receive her, offering his assistance as far as it would go. But Lydia was determined to be married and cared not when. Since such were her feelings, it only remained, he thought, to secure and expedite a marriage which, in his very first conversation with Wickham, he easily learnt had never been *his* design. They met several times, for there was much to be discussed. Wickham, of course, wanted more than he could get, but at length was induced to be reasonable.

Nothing was to be done that Mr Darcy did not do

himself. Your uncle and Mr Darcy battled it together for a long time, but at last your uncle was forced to yield. Instead of being allowed to be of use to his niece, Mr Gardiner was forced to put up with only being given the credit for it.

The contents of this letter throw you into a flutter of spirits. Your heart whispers that he did it for you, but it is a hope shortly checked by other considerations, and you soon feel that even *your* vanity is insufficient, when required to depend on his affection for you – for a woman who had already refused him – as able to overcome a sentiment so natural as abhorrence against relationship with Wickham. Brother-in-law of Wickham! Every kind of pride must revolt from the connection.

The day of Wickham and Lydia's departure soon comes, and your mother is forced to submit to a separation which is likely to continue at least a twelvemonth. Peace once again returns to Longbourn, and you must now do your best to put Mr Darcy from your mind.

A week after Lydia and Wickham's departure, you receive an invitation from the Philipses to join them on a trip to Bath.

If you feel you might benefit from some time away from your family after recent events, turn to page 165 to accept the invitation.

If you are tired of all these trips away and would rather rest quietly at home, turn to page 214.

*Y*ou refuse Captain Wentworth, to his great and evident distress. He can hardly believe that you have broken his heart again, in exactly the same way that you did three years ago. You can hardly believe it either, and hurry away as soon as you can.

You return home to Longbourn at the earliest opportunity and open your heart to Jane, whose concern and astonishment are equal at hearing all that has passed in Bath. When you retire to bed at night, you wonder what will become of you both, and whether Mr Bingley will ever come back for Jane. Since Lydia's marriage to Wickham, your hopes have diminished. No matter how much he might have loved Jane, and indeed might still love her, it seems unlikely to you that Bingley would ever willingly attach himself to a family with such a recent scandal marring its name.

Recalling the scandal naturally leads your thoughts once again to Mr Darcy, to whom your whole family will forever be in debt for his part in securing Lydia's marriage. You have heard nothing of him since and have done your best to put hopes of ever seeing him again, and the idea that he might have helped Lydia for your sake alone, far from your mind. If Bingley, who has nothing like Darcy's reasons, is unlikely to associate with you after the scandal, it is hardly possible that Darcy ever could. It is with difficulty that you at last put these troubling reflections to the back of your mind and fall asleep.

Proceed to page 172.

You accept his proposal and are married soon after. Captain Wentworth is an attentive and affectionate husband, you glory in being a sailor's wife, and only dread of a future war can dim your sunshine.

THE END

Congratulations. You have successfully completed your mission.

The next morning, before you have a chance to tell your aunt and uncle the truth about Mr Bennet, you are distracted by the arrival in Bath of your cousins Charles and Mary Musgrove, and the Harvilles from Lyme. You are obliged to be with the Musgroves from breakfast to dinner, and when you arrive you find that Captain Wentworth is also with them. When he sees you, he looks as grave as he did when he left the concert and just two minutes after your entering the room, he turns to Captain Harville and says, 'We will write the letter we were talking of, Harville, now, if you will give me materials.'

The materials are all at hand on a separate table, which Captain Wentworth makes his way to and, nearly turning his back on you all, sits down and is engrossed by writing.

While the others all talk gaily of Louisa and Benwick's forthcoming marriage, Captain Harville leaves his seat and, moving to a window, invites you to join him. You discuss the engagement between Captain Benwick and Louisa and find yourself debating whether it is men or women who are the more faithful lovers. Captain Harville observes to you that he has never in his life opened a book which didn't have something to say about woman's inconstancy. You are not impressed with this argument.

'Yes, but they were all written by men!' you retort. 'Men have had every advantage of us in telling their own story. Education has been theirs in so much higher a degree; the pen has been in their hands. I will not allow books to prove anything.'

'We shall never agree upon this question,' Captain Harville begins to say, when a slight noise calls your attention to Captain Wentworth. It is nothing more than that his pen has fallen down; but you are half inclined to suspect that the pen only fell because he was occupied by you, and striving to catch sounds, which you do not think he could have caught. You cannot deny that there is part of you that hopes he *did* hear you.

You turn your attention back to Captain Harville and assure him that you believe men such as him to be capable of everything great and good in their married lives, so long as the woman they love lives, and lives for them.

'All the privilege I claim for my own sex,' you add, '(it is not a very enviable one; you need not covet it), is that of loving longest, when existence or when hope is gone.'

'You are a good soul,' cries Captain Harville, putting his hand on your arm, quite affectionately. 'There is no quarrelling with you. And when I think of Benwick, my tongue is tied.'

At that moment you are interrupted by the arrival of Captain Benwick himself, accompanied by Louisa and her parents. They have come for the Harvilles, whom they wish to take on a tour of their favourite spots in Bath. You are all to meet again this evening, and Louisa and Captain Benwick express their pleasure at the prospect of having a greater opportunity to talk to you once again and catch up on all that has passed since you were last together, at Lyme. The Harvilles are ready to go and are only waiting on Captain Wentworth, who seals his letter with great rapidity, and is then ready. It seems to you that he even has a hurried, agitated air, which shows impatience to be gone, as if not wishing to be left alone with only you and the Musgroves. You have the kindest 'Good morning, God bless you!' from Captain Harville, but not a word, nor even a *look,* from Captain Wentworth.

You turn towards the table where he has been writing so as to conceal your disappointed expression from the Musgroves and are endeavouring to recover your spirits when you hear footsteps returning. The door opens, and Captain Wentworth himself comes back into the room. He begs your pardon, but he forgot his gloves, and he instantly crosses the room to the writing table, draws out a letter from under the scattered paper, places it before you, looks at you with eyes of entreaty for a time, before hastily collecting his gloves and once again leaving the room.

You are astonished indeed: while writing his letter of instruction, it seems he was also addressing *you.*

You hastily open the letter with trembling hands and your eyes devour his words. He has been listening to you and Captain Harville half in agony and half in hope. He prays that he is not too late, and offers himself to you again with a heart even more your own than when you almost broke it, three years ago. He has loved none but you – unjust he has been, weak and resentful too, but never inconstant – and you alone have brought him back to Bath. Uncertain of his fate, he will return to the Musgroves' lodgings as soon as possible and 'A word, a look,' he concludes, 'will be enough to decide whether I will see you again this evening or never.'

You are overwhelmed with surprise and happiness and go after the Captain at once. You catch up with him and, for the second time in your life, he makes you a proposal of marriage.

If you wish to accept, turn to page 192.

Alternatively, if it suddenly dawns on you that though you have always secretly loved Captain Wentworth and longed for him to forgive you, in actual fact all you really wanted was his forgiveness, and besides, you are not sure that you could really bear the anxiety that would come with being married to a captain of the navy, then turn to page 191 to do your best to get out of a truly awkward situation.

As you walk across the lawn towards the river, you turn back to look again; and to your very great surprise, the owner of it himself suddenly comes forward from the road which leads behind it to the stables.

Your eyes instantly meet, and both of you blush. He absolutely starts, and for a moment seems immovable from surprise; but shortly recovering himself, advances towards your party, and speaks to you, if not in terms of perfect composure, at least of perfect civility.

Astonished and confused, you scarcely dare lift your eyes to his face, and know not what answer you return to his civil enquiries after your family. His manner is greatly improved from what it was when you last parted at Rosings, and you are amazed at the alteration. Every sentence that he utters increases your embarrassment; and every idea of the impropriety of your being found here recurs to your mind.

The few minutes in which you continue together are some of the most uncomfortable of your life. Nor does he seem much more at ease: when he speaks, his accent has none of its usual sedateness; and he repeats his enquiries as to the time of your having left Longbourn, and of your stay in Derbyshire, so often, and in so hurried a way, as plainly speaks the distraction of his thoughts. At length every idea seems to fail him; and, after standing a few moments without saying a word, he suddenly recollects himself, and takes leave.

The others then join you, and, wholly engrossed by your own feelings, you follow them in silence. You are overpowered by shame and vexation. How strange must your being there appear to him! You blush again and again over the perverseness of the meeting. And his behaviour, so strikingly altered – what can it mean? That he should even speak to you is amazing! But to speak with such civility, to enquire after your family! Never in your life have you seen his manners so easy, never has he spoken with such gentleness as on this unexpected meeting. What a contrast it offers to his last address in Rosings Park, when he put his letter into your hand! You know not what to think, nor how to account for it.

You long to know in what manner he thinks of you. Whether he feels more of pain or of pleasure in seeing you, you cannot tell, but his parting suggests that he certainly does not see you with composure.

At length, the remarks of your companions on your absence of mind rouse you, and you feel the necessity of appearing more like yourself.

After walking for some time, you are making your way back towards the house on the opposite side of the river when you are again surprised by the sight of Mr Darcy approaching you, and at no great distance. You resolve to appear and to speak with calmness but in truth, your nerves are greatly discomposed.

With a glance you see that he has lost none of his recent civility; and, to imitate his politeness, you begin as you meet to admire the beauty of the place; but you have not got beyond the words 'delightful' and 'charming' when some unlucky recollections obtrude and you fancy that praise of Pemberley might make it seem as if you are, after all, hoping to become mistress of it! Your colour changes, and you say no more.

He asks if you will do him the honour of introducing him to your friends. You can hardly suppress a smile at his now seeking the acquaintance of some of those very relations against whom his pride had revolted in his offer to you.

The introduction, however, is immediately made; and as you name their relationship to yourself, you steal a sly look at him, to see how he bears it. That he is *surprised* by the connection is evident from his expression; he sustains it, however, with fortitude, and, so far from decamping as fast as he can from such disgraceful companions, turns back with you, and enters into conversation with Mr Gardiner. You listen most attentively to all that passes between them, and glory in every expression, every sentence of your uncle's which marks his intelligence, his taste and his good manners.

The conversation soon turns upon fishing; and you hear Mr Darcy invite him to fish there as often as he chooses while he continues in the neighbourhood, offering at the same time to supply him with fishing tackle, and pointing out those parts of the stream where there is usually most sport. Your astonishment at his generosity is extreme.

Continually you repeat to yourself, 'Why is he so altered? From what can it proceed? It cannot be for *me* – it cannot be for *my* sake that his manners are thus softened.'

After walking some time in this way Mrs Gardiner goes to take her husband's arm and Mr Darcy takes her place by you as you walk. After a short silence, you speak. You wish him to know that you had been assured of his absence before you came to the place. He acknowledges that he was unexpected, and says that business with his steward had occasioned his coming forward a few hours before the rest of the party with whom he was travelling. 'They will join me early tomorrow,' he continues, 'and among them are some who will claim an acquaintance with you – Mr Bingley and his sisters.'

You remember the last time Mr Bingley was spoken of between you, and the colour rises in your cheeks.

'But there is also one other person in the party who more particularly wishes to be known to you,' continues Mr Darcy. 'Will you allow me, or do I ask too much, to introduce my sister to your acquaintance during your stay at Lambton?'

The surprise of such an application is great indeed; it is too great for you to know in what manner you consent to it. You feel sincerely honoured.

You now walk on in silence, each of you deep in thought. You are so surprised, so pleased by his change in manner, and cannot help but wonder what he means by it. You want to believe that it is all for your benefit, that his feelings for you have not been entirely extinguished, but you chastise yourself for having such foolish hopes and thoughts. When you reach the carriage you are all pressed to go into the house and take some refreshment; but this is declined, and you part on each side with the utmost politeness. Mr Darcy hands you and your aunt into the carriage; and when it drives off, you see him walk slowly towards the house.

The observations of your uncle and aunt begin; and each pronounces Darcy to be infinitely superior to anything they had expected. Mrs Gardiner cannot reconcile Wickham's account of Darcy and his cruelty with what she has seen of the man himself. Now that you are alone, you give them to understand, in as guarded a manner as you can without actually naming your authority, the nature of what you learnt from Mr Darcy, omitting the details concerning his sister. Mrs Gardiner is surprised and concerned; and when she has come to accept it, she regrets ever having seen Darcy in a bad light.

The rest of the day is spent with Mrs Gardiner's former acquaintances, but you have little attention for any of these new friends: you can do nothing but think, and think with wonder, of Mr Darcy's civility, and above all, of his wishing you to be acquainted with his sister. Whatever desire Miss Darcy might have of being acquainted with you must be the work of her brother, and without looking further, it is satisfactory; it is gratifying to know that his resentment has not made him think really ill of you.

The very next day Mr Darcy brings his sister to visit you, and with astonishment you see that your new acquaintance is at least as embarrassed as you are. Since being at Lambton you had heard that Miss Darcy was exceedingly proud, but the observation of a few minutes convinces you that she is only exceedingly shy. She is less handsome than her brother, but there is sense and good humour in her face, and her manners are perfectly unassuming and gentle. You had expected to find her as acute and unembarrassed an observer as Mr Darcy once was, and are very much relieved by discerning such different feelings.

You are interrupted by Mr Bingley, who has likewise come to wait on you. Upon seeing him, your thoughts naturally fly to your sister and you quickly perceive that his do too when he observes to you, in a tone which has something of real regret, that it was 'a very long time since he had had the pleasure of seeing Jane', adding quickly, 'It is above eight months. We have not met since the 26th of November, when we were all dancing together at Netherfield.'

It is clear to you that Miss Darcy is not a rival for Jane.

It is not often that you can turn your eyes on Mr Darcy himself; but whenever you do, you are pleased by what you see. Never, even in the company of his dear friends at Netherfield, or his dignified relations at Rosings, have you seen him so desirous to please as now, when no importance can result from the success of his endeavours.

When they arise to depart, your visitors invite you to dinner. Mrs Gardiner looks at you, but you have turned away your head in momentary embarrassment. She ventures to engage for your attendance, and the day after the next is fixed on.

Eager to be alone, and fearful of enquiries or hints from your uncle and aunt, you stay with them only long enough to hear their favourable opinion of Bingley, and then hurry away to dress.

Your aunt suggests that you must return the politeness of Miss Darcy's early visit by calling on her the following morning. You are pleased; though when you ask yourself the reason, you have very little to say in reply.

You set off soon after breakfast, and on reaching the house are shown through the hall into a saloon where you are received most civilly by Miss Darcy. By Mrs Hurst and Miss Bingley you are noticed only by a curtsy, but even they cannot dampen your high spirits.

Fruit and cake are served, and not long afterwards Mr Darcy enters the room. No sooner does he appear than you wisely resolve to be perfectly easy and unembarrassed – a resolution the more necessary to be made because you see that the suspicions of the whole party are awakened against you both. Miss Darcy, on her brother's entrance, exerts herself much more to talk; and you see that he is anxious for you and his sister to get acquainted, and forwards as much as possible every attempt at conversation on either side. Miss Bingley sees all this likewise; and, with seeming jealousy, takes the first opportunity of saying, with sneering civility, 'Pray, Miss Eliza, are not the Hertfordshire militia removed from Meryton? They must be a great loss to *your* family.'

You instantly comprehend that she means Wickham, and the various recollections connected with him give you a moment's distress; but exerting yourself vigorously to repel the ill-natured attack, you confirm that the militia have indeed left Meryton, answering the question in a tolerably disengaged tone.

Darcy, with a heightened complexion, earnestly looks at you, and his sister, her thoughts evidently flying to her attempted elopement with Wickham, is overcome with confusion and unable to lift up her eyes. Even Miss Bingley, if she knew what pain she was then giving her beloved friend, would undoubtedly have refrained from the hint.

Your visit does not continue long after this question and answer, and Mr Darcy attends you to your carriage. You return to Lambton, and on your way, you and your aunt talk of all that occurred during your visit, except the very thing that most interests you both. The looks and behaviour of everybody is discussed, except of the person who mostly engaged your attention. You talk of his sister, his friends, his house, his fruit, of everything but himself; yet you long to know what Mrs Gardiner thinks of him, and Mrs Gardiner would be highly gratified if only you'd begin the subject.

Continue on page 181.

'*I*s there no one to help me?' are the first words which burst from Captain Wentworth, in a tone of despair.

'Rub her hands, rub her temples,' you cry; 'here are salts: take them, take them.'

Louisa is raised up and supported more firmly between them. Everything is done that you prompted, but in vain. Captain Wentworth, staggering against the wall for his support, exclaims in the bitterest agony, 'Oh God! Her father and mother! How is the news to be broken?'

'A surgeon!' you cry. 'Captain Benwick, you must know where a surgeon is to be found?'

Captain Benwick resigns the poor corpse-like figure entirely to Charles's care, and sets off for the town with the utmost rapidity.

'Lizzy, Lizzy,' cries Charles, 'what is to be done next? What, in heaven's name, is to be done next?'

Captain Wentworth's eyes are also turned towards you.

You instruct them to carry her gently to the inn, and you are making your way thither when you are met at the end of the Cobb by Captain Harville, who insists that Louisa be taken to his house to await the surgeon.

The surgeon is with you almost before it seems possible. You are all sick with worry while he examines her. He is by no means hopeless, however, and though her head received a severe contusion, he has seen greater injuries recovered from.

The tone, the look, with which 'Thank God!' is uttered

by Captain Wentworth, is something you are sure you will never forget. His love for Louisa is clear.

It is agreed that Mary and Charles should stay with Louisa, and Captain Wentworth is to carry the news to her parents after returning you to Bath. During your journey, Captain Wentworth is silent. Once only does he exclaim out loud, 'Oh God! That I had not given way to her at the fatal moment! Had I done as I ought! But so eager and so resolute! Dear, sweet Louisa!'

You wonder whether it ever occurs to him, now, to question the justness of his own previous opinion as to the universal felicity and advantage of firmness of character; and whether it might not strike him that, like all other qualities of the mind, it should have its proportions and limits. You think it can scarcely escape him to feel that a persuadable temper might sometimes be as much in favour of happiness as a very resolute character.

You get on fast and are at Bath by dusk, where Captain Wentworth takes leave of you to make the distressing communication to Louisa's parents, before returning to Lyme.

You explain all to your aunt and uncle, who are greatly concerned for Louisa's welfare, and are anxious lest you should have suffered from the distress yourself. You assure them that you are quite well, and are only in need of a little rest. You retire early to bed, and though your mind is full of the events of the past few days, and thoughts of Wentworth and Louisa, you are so fatigued that it is not long before you fall into a deep and uninterrupted sleep.

𝒴ou receive an encouraging account from Lyme the following afternoon: Louisa shows signs of consciousness and the intervals of sense are longer. Captain Wentworth remains at Lyme and you believe it is only a matter of time before his engagement to Louisa is announced. You steel yourself to receive the news as best you can, and once again immerse yourself wholeheartedly in life at Bath so that you won't have time to reflect on it.

To your very great surprise, you find that the very Mr Bennet whom you passed at Lyme has been for some time in Bath, and been so attentive to the Philipses, shown such readiness to apologise for the past, that their former good understanding has been completely re-established and Mr Bennet forgiven completely.

You soon meet Mr Bennet again, and he is greatly surprised to discover that the pretty girl he saw at Lyme is none other than his own cousin. He is quite as good-looking as he appeared at Lyme, his countenance improves by speaking, and his manners are exactly what they ought to be. You converse easily and are delighted with your new acquaintance. You could not have supposed it possible that you could feel happy in *anyone's* company so soon after resigning yourself to Wentworth's love for Louisa, let alone the company of a handsome and agreeable gentleman such as Mr Bennet.

Your attachment grows daily; and you are so frequently together, so frequently seen to be pleased with each other, that though you are unaware of it till much later, your perceived intimacy gives rise to the general expectation of an imminent engagement between you. You really do like Mr Bennet, and your attachment advances so rapidly that you do not think it will be long before you are quite in love with him.

About this time you receive a letter from Mary which gives you fresh and astonishing news of Louisa. She is well enough recovered to have returned home, whither she has gone with Charles, Mary and, to everyone's astonishment, Captain Benwick, who is in love with Louisa and set to marry her before the month is out. You have never in your life been more surprised.

Captain Benwick and Louisa Musgrove! And Captain Wentworth is free still! You are once again thrown into a state of turmoil and know not what to make of your many contradictory feelings.

The following day you are taking a walk about Bath with Mr Bennet when it begins to rain. You turn in to a coffee shop, while Mr Bennet goes in search of a carriage. As you sit near the window waiting for him, you discern, most decidedly and distinctly, Captain Wentworth walking down the street. You almost jump in surprise and hope that nobody has perceived you start. As you try to recover your senses, Captain Wentworth enters.

He is clearly struck and confused by the sight of you and looks quite red. Mutual enquiries on common subjects are made, but you are both so distracted that neither of you is much the wiser for what you hear. He is much less at ease than formerly; and you cannot help wondering if this consciousness springs from a change in his sentiments towards you.

'Though I came only yesterday,' he says after a short pause, 'I have equipped myself properly for Bath already, you see' (pointing to a new umbrella); 'I wish you would make use of it, if you are determined to walk; though I think it would be more prudent to let me get you a chair.'

You hurriedly decline it all, sure that the rain will come to nothing in the end, and tell him that you are only waiting for your cousin Mr Bennet to arrive with a carriage.

You have hardly spoken the words when Mr Bennet walks in. In another moment you walk off together, your arm under his, and with a somewhat embarrassed glance you turn back to Captain Wentworth and only have time to bid him good morning. You regret that you were obliged to part with Captain Wentworth so soon, and cannot help wishing Mr Bennet had taken longer in returning. Captain Wentworth's kindness towards you was not unfelt, however, and as the carriage takes you home you feel yourself glowing with the feelings which such attentions naturally excited.

The following evening the Philipses invite you to accompany them to a concert. As you are waiting in the Octagon Room for some ladies of your aunt's acquaintance, the door opens and Captain Wentworth walks in.

He does not look unhappy to see you, and approaches you and begins his polite enquiries.

After talking of the weather, Bath, and the concert, your conversation begins to flag. You are trying to think of something to say when Captain Wentworth, without any introduction, suddenly expresses his surprise at the unexpected engagement between Louisa and Benwick. You do not immediately know what to say in reply. You had previously thought Captain Wentworth very much in love with Louisa, but from the way he speaks of her it would seem that his feelings were never that deep. You are pleased to hear it.

Just at that moment, Mr Bennet arrives, and you are necessarily divided from Captain Wentworth for a moment to make your greeting. When you turn back he is gone, and you feel that it is extremely unlucky once again to have been so untimely interrupted by Mr Bennet. Though you know it is unkind, you cannot help somewhat regretting your relation's presence at the concert this evening.

You take your place in the concert room and Mr Bennet sits by you. You had thought yourself almost in love with Mr Bennet, but it dawns on you now that while Captain Wentworth is in the room there can be no thinking of Mr Bennet.

The first act finishes and towards the end of the interval you catch sight of Captain Wentworth again. By very slow degrees he comes at last near enough to speak to you. He begins by speaking of the concert and he even goes so far as to look down towards the bench, as if about to sit down; but at that very moment Mr Bennet begs your pardon, but you 'must be applied to' to explain the Italian words of the previous song.

You hastily do your best to explain the words to Mr Bennet, and when you turn again to Captain Wentworth he makes a hurried sort of farewell, insisting that he must get home as fast as he can.

'Is not this song worth staying for?' you say, anxious for him not to leave so soon.

'No!' he replies impressively, 'there is nothing worth my staying for,' and he is gone directly.

You are struck by his angry tone and cannot immediately account for it. And then all at once it occurs to you: Captain Wentworth is jealous of Mr Bennet! It is the only intelligible motive. For a moment the gratification is exquisite indeed, but very different thoughts quickly succeed. How is the truth to reach him that you feel nothing for Mr Bennet? It is misery to think of your cousin's attentions now; their evil is incalculable.

The following day you are engaged to visit an old childhood friend by the name of Mrs Smith, who now permanently resides in Bath. She has heard rumours that you are soon to be engaged to Mr Bennet and when you assure her that there is no foundation to them she is most heartily relieved. She proceeds to tell you that Mr Bennet, far from being rich, has been cut off by his father, is in great debt, and seeks to marry his way into solvency again. Though you are far from rich yourself, by marrying you he would ingratiate himself once more within the Bennet family, by which means he hopes to appease his father and reclaim the fortune due to him. You thank her most gratefully for the information, and chide yourself for being seduced by his flattery. You have now an even greater reason to regret the attentions which are threatening to ruin, once again (and perhaps for evermore), your hopes with Captain Wentworth.

Continue on page 193.

𝒴ou politely turn down the Philipses' invitation, and settle back into everyday life at Longbourn. You do your best to put Mr Darcy from your mind, but after learning what he has done for Lydia and Wickham, it is not an easy task.

Proceed to page 172.

*T*he gardener takes you across the park to the handsome woodlands, along a path that winds along the perimeter, and then along the riverbank back up to the house. You see and admire it all with great pleasure, and the gardener is able to tell you the history of the estate, which your aunt and uncle find of great interest. You cannot quite give him your full attention, however, as your mind is somewhat distracted by memories of another history, told to you by both Darcy and Wickham.

When you have finished your tour you thank the gardener for his time, return to the carriage and take your leave of Pemberley, conscious of the fact that Darcy himself arrives tomorrow and once again thankful that your journey was not by any circumstance delayed a day.

You turn out of the park and on to the road to Lambton. Your companions talk little, tired from their walk, and you are therefore at liberty to indulge the melancholy reflections that the day has given rise to.

It is hard not to think of Darcy arriving, hard not to think that he will be within five miles of you from tomorrow, and hard not to wish that you could see him again and make him understand the very great change which your feelings have undergone since you last saw him. You wish him to understand how earnestly you regret blaming him for ruining Wickham's happiness, and to show him that, since reading his letter, you now have a fuller understanding of the situation and you no longer bear him any ill will for his part in harming Jane's.

As your thoughts turn to Jane you are once more reminded that she has not written to you for a number of days and you are just beginning to wonder with concern why that could be when you hear the driver call 'Look out!', and at that moment you are run off the road by another carriage. You are thrown from your seat as your vehicle overturns and lands, upside down, crumpled by its own weight, in the ditch by the side of the road. With great difficulty, and suffering from the shock and a number of broken bones, do you manage to crawl from the wreckage, making your way through the shattered carriage window, in great and overwhelming pain. When you have to some degree recovered your senses, your first thought is for your aunt and uncle. You call their names but there is no answer and you fear that they are trapped within the wreckage. You call for help, hoping that someone from the other carriage will come to your aid, and to your great joy and relief, you hear the sound of footsteps approaching. You turn your head to see what knight in shining armour is coming your way and to your great and all-encompassing horror, see only Miss Bingley.

'Good afternoon, Miss Bennet,' says she, looming over you with a smile of sneering and wholly inappropriate civility.

Terror grips you.

'I had heard that you were in the area. I was forced to rest and wait in a most squalid little inn at Lambton while my driver made a small repair to the carriage. Imagine my surprise when I happened to overhear one of the servants mentioning that Mr and Mrs Gardiner and their niece

Miss Bennet were out for the day visiting *Pemberley*!'

You try to move but she stops you with a well-placed foot on your chest.

'Mr Darcy has been speaking of you a great deal too much lately, Miss Bennet. I won't stand for it. Who knows what witchcraft you have employed to catch his attention? Though you have made an impression of sorts, do you think such a man as Mr Darcy could ever seriously consider someone like you? Do you think he could ever be induced to marry a woman without family, connections, fortune, beauty or taste?'

You open your mouth to reply, but before you have a chance she screams at you, 'Not if I have anything to do with it!' And with that she returns to her carriage. You use all your strength to try and crawl out of the road, but your injuries are great and it is more than you can manage. Miss Bingley comes at you with great speed, runs over your already broken body, and hurtles off in the direction of Pemberley, leaving you for dead. Her methods are effective, and with a broken back and many internal injuries, it is not long before your consciousness slips away from you and into the welcoming arms of death.

THE END

*Unfortunately, you have failed
to complete your mission.*

You try not to worry about it and do your best to get back to sleep. At last you are successful and you wake in the morning as happy as you were when you first took to your bed, and not even your mother can have any effect on your high spirits.

When you next see Mr Darcy you ask him playfully to account for his ever having fallen in love with you.

'My beauty you had early withstood, and as for my manners – my behaviour to *you* was at least always bordering on the uncivil, and I never spoke to you without rather wishing to give you pain than not. Now be sincere; did you admire me for my impertinence?'

'For the liveliness of your mind, I did,' replies your husband-to-be.

And so it continues, each of you light-heartedly teasing the other. You have a joint wedding with your sister Jane and happy is the day on which your mother sees her two most deserving daughters married. With what delighted pride she afterwards visits Mrs Bingley and talks of Mrs Darcy may be guessed. Mr Bingley buys an estate in the neighbouring county to Derbyshire and you and Jane, in addition to every other source of happiness, are within thirty miles of each other. You invite Kitty to stay with you often, and in society so superior to what she had generally known, her improvement is great. Mary stays at home and when no longer mortified by comparisons between her sisters' beauty and her own, mixes more with the world than she was wont. Though Wickham can never be received at

Pemberley, for your sake, Mr Darcy assists him further in his profession, and Lydia is an occasional visitor when her husband is away enjoying himself in London or Bath.

Miss Bingley is deeply mortified by Darcy's marriage, but as she thinks it advisable to retain the right of visiting Pemberley, she drops all her resentment, is fonder than ever of Georgiana and endeavours to make up for all prior incivility to you.

Lady Catherine, having been extremely indignant when she first learnt of your engagement, sends a letter so very abusive, especially of you, that at first all intercourse is put to an end. At length, you persuade your husband to overlook the offence and seek a reconciliation. At last her resentment gives way and either out of affection for him, or curiosity to see how you conduct yourself, she condescends to wait on you at Pemberley, in spite of the pollution which its woods have received, not merely from the presence of such a mistress as yourself, but the visits of all your inferior connections.

With the Gardiners you are always on the most intimate terms and both you and Mr Darcy feel the warmest gratitude towards them as the persons who, by bringing you into Derbyshire, were the means of uniting you at last.

THE END

Congratulations. You have successfully completed your mission.

You rise from your bed and go to the window, in the hope that you will be able to clear your mind. It is dark, but the grey light from the moon illuminates the garden. All is still, all is peaceful. Your mind, by contrast, is in turmoil. You try to gather your thoughts, but you cannot. Why, if you are happy, do you feel so ill at ease? The only man on earth who could make you happy has said he wants to marry you, and you have accepted him. Everything is set for your happiness if only you could submit to it. You want so desperately to do so, and yet you know there is something wrong. You try to comfort yourself, to imagine your future life of happiness with Mr Darcy, but though you foresee happiness in the months immediately ahead, your confidence falters when you try to look beyond them. Pemberley is beautiful, no doubt, and your husband-to-be quite the most remarkable man you have ever met; your library will be vast and diverting – but something about this picture does not sit comfortably.

Just what on earth are you going to do with your days once you're married? What will you and your husband talk about? Will you forever be going over the unlikely circumstances under which you met and (at last) fell in love? Will you go on reminding one another of how it was in the beginning until long after you have ceased to feel anything but indifference for each other? Familiarity breeds contempt, and Pemberley is a long way from Hertfordshire; who can say how often your friends and family will be able to visit you and diversify the domestic scene? You reassure yourself that even if these fears are just, before long, perhaps, you will have children, and their care will sufficiently divert you. You take comfort in this, until a vision of your mother comes before you, and you feel that to live solely for your children is no life at all. God forbid you should turn out like your mother.

You tell yourself these doubts are only natural and dismiss them as best you can, but still your mind is ill at ease. Something deeper is yet troubling you, but still you know not what it is. Could it have been something you read? With little hope of finding an answer there, but at a loss for what else to do, you make your way down to the library. In the light afforded you by your low-burning candle you scan the shelves for those titles you have read most recently, and take down a number of volumes. You flick through the first that comes to hand, hoping to find something that will prompt your memory and bring to the fore that which yet lingers at the back of your mind; but no such discovery befriends you. You take up a second volume, and a third, desperately searching your mind, trying to think what it might be that could have remained with you on some deep level, though you were not at first aware of it. Still you find nothing. You go back to the shelves and take down volume after volume – all your favourite novels, all those works which you have treasured over these last years – until you are surrounded by a sea of books, spread out around you as you sit on the library floor in the quiet of the half-light.

You are still for some moments, unsure of what to do. And slowly at first, but then all at once, it begins to dawn on you. A wave of realisation washes over you with the most awful force. You take up the book nearest to hand and skip to the end, to those most treasured passages where the heroine is finally united with the man she loves. He makes her a proposal of marriage, she accepts it and the story ends happily. You pick up another title. The same is true here. You hastily take up volume after volume, only to discover the same devastating truth in all of them: the moment the heroine of the narrative agrees to wed, the book comes to a swift end. Following every happy marriage are the words 'The End', stamped most authoritatively upon the page.

'Good God!' you think to yourself. 'And is this the fate that awaits me also? If I marry Mr Darcy, will I, too, face "The End"?' Apparently there is nothing that can follow the marriages of your favourite heroines – no story worth telling, no circumstance worth reading; all is apparently devoid of interest. Their adventure and excitement are over; they cease to be of interest to anyone.

A thousand feelings rush upon you at once, and your world seems to close in around you. What you stand to gain upon your marriage to Mr Darcy is great indeed, but what must you sacrifice? What must be given up for this match to take place? Not just your name, but your very *existence* as Elizabeth Bennet. Every book that surrounds you seems to be forcing you to the same conclusion, the same distressing realisation: that marriage will be 'The End' for you. Are you ready for it? Are you ready for the end of the adventure – ready to say goodbye to all in life that might be worth writing or reading about?

Never before have you been so distraught, so torn, so at a loss. What is to be your fate? You must make the final choice, the choice of all choices. Are you prepared to sign yourself over to this new life, to disappear from notice, to cease to be of interest, to cease to be Elizabeth Bennet and become, instead, Mrs Darcy?

The shock of your realisation is great, and you know not how many hours you sit there in the darkness amongst your books (your candle long since burnt out) before at last climbing heavily and wearily back to your bed to steal what repose you can before the new day begins.

When you awake but a few hours later, it is with a very heavy feeling. Jane's shock at your distressed appearance is great. Through many tears, and with great difficulty, you tell her that you cannot, you must not marry Mr Darcy. Though he is the man most likely to bring you happiness of any man you are ever likely to meet, you must give him up; another fate awaits you. You know not how the news is to be broken to him, but know you cannot see him yourself. To be the cause of so much distress to him is almost enough to break your heart entirely and you do not have the strength for it.

Jane arranges it all. You are to be conveyed by your father's carriage to London, to your aunt, your dear aunt

Gardiner, to whom she sends word by the first morning's post. All is commotion at Longbourn. Your father is perplexed and concerned, your mother is distracted. That you could have secured the hand of the richest man of your acquaintance only to throw it away again the next day seems to her the most wilful obstinacy, and she immediately takes to her bed in a fit of nerves. It is left to Jane to take the news to Mr Darcy, and with the help of Mr Bingley the deed is done while you are already on your way to London. You know not what grief he feels on the occasion for you never ask Jane, and the matter is never spoken of between you again.

You arrive in London, and, your sister's letter having only just preceded you, are welcomed into the arms of your aunt, who mercifully spares you questions. You talk and eat but little that night, and are grateful for the silent understanding shown to you by your aunt and uncle. You do little more than rest in your first weeks there, but you know that in time your spirits will be restored. You know what you must do, and as the pain begins to subside, your strength grows. Agonising though it was, you *know* you made the right decision and this conviction supports you through the darkest hours.

You alone know it at present, but the night you spent amongst your books was significant for more than one reason: you knew soon enough that you could never marry Mr Darcy, but with this surprising discovery came a second realisation, no less startling than the first, and you knew there and then what you must do instead. That night, you realised that you *yourself* must write.

On the Monday morning of your sixth week at Gracechurch Street you wake with a strong sense of purpose. After breakfast, you make your excuses and go to the drawing room. You sit down at the writing table, draw out a pen and a blank sheet of paper, and prepare to write the first page of your book. Drawing heavily on your own experiences over these last few years, you plan to write about the adventures of a young woman in pursuit of the right match. Unlike the volumes that lay before you that fateful night, however, *your* book will not send out the message that Woman's only choice is to marry – and that her story will end the moment she does so. You are determined to find a way for your heroine to say 'no' to 'The End' and continue her adventure. You dip your pen in your ink, put pen to paper and begin to write as follows:

Continue on page ix.

ACKNOWLEDGEMENTS

I would like to thank Louisa Joyner at Faber for fondly remembering the original edition and giving it a new life in its current form; Henry Eliot for wielding the editorial knife with the skill of a surgeon and eye of a sculptor; Helen Bleck for her incisive copy edits; and Sara O'Keeffe at Nurnberg Associates for her advocacy and encouragement.

I would also like to thank Adam Chase for his unwavering support; Mum and Dad for their love and guidance; Eliza and Amelia for their love and encouragement; and Catriona Ward for more years of literary friendship than I care to admit.

Lastly, I would like to thank Jane Austen for the legacy she bequeathed us, these six jewels of the canon that continue to shine light in even the most uncertain of times.